An Item from
The Late News

By the same author
Girl with a Monkey
A Descant for Gossips
The Well Dressed Explorer
The Slow Natives
A Boatload of Home Folk
The Acolyte
A Kindness Cup
Hunting the Wild Pineapple

An Item from
The Late News

THEA ASTLEY

University of Queensland Press
St Lucia • London • New York

Published by the University of Queensland Press, St Lucia, Queensland 1982

Typeset by University of Queensland Press
Printed and bound by Hedges & Bell Pty Ltd, Melbourne

Distributed in the United Kingdom, Europe, the Middle East, Africa, and the Caribbean by Prentice-Hall International, International Book Distributors Ltd, 66 Wood Lane End, Hemel Hempstead, Herts., England.

Published with the assistance of the Literature Board of the Australia Council.

National Library of Australia
Cataloguing-in-Publication data

Astley, Thea, 1925– .
   An item from the late news.
   ISBN 0 7022 1702 6.

   I. Title (Series: Paperback prose).

A823'.3

Library of Congress Cataloguing in Publication Data
Astley, Thea.
   An item from the late news.

   I. Title.
PR9619.3.A7518   1982   823   82-11177
ISBN 0-7022-1702-6

There will be no hope for man until he returns to the caves.
Higher phases are reached by exaltation, illusion, fanaticism.

Simone Weil.

It all came to a head in a couple of months, really, those two months ten years ago now when the town prepared for and then dismissed its barbaric Christmas. And why barbaric? Always barbaric?

Not always, I suppose, though the beer-gut belchings and the rattle of schooner glasses that always discover the Christmas crib and soothe the infant with whack yoicks, seem to me to have a muckworm style. All towns. Not just this one. Because this one is smaller, a mere speck on the world's glassy eye, the grossness is horribly apparent.

Time usually diminishes the memory; but for me it has done nothing but magnify that swollen moment of history when Wafer had the wax on his wings melted from flying too close, not to the sun, but to the local grandees.

I look back. I was. I am. I am now. Very now. I was then.

There was nothing outside that town.

Is nothing.

Can nothing be walled by nothing?

If I stand, in memory's shade only, under the tin awnings of the council chambers and swivel through the compass quarters, the north lurches up in a side-swipe

1

of scrubby range glinting with imagined Eldorados. I say "imagined" for their glittering non-presence was part of the corruption. West, scrub careered into salt-bush into desert. South, a lost landscape of salt-pans. I swivel unsteadily as I travel each landscape until my face smashes against the sapless timbers of the building — the slowly creaking fan, the general store's wall calendar of a beach like a fable, the filing baskets — seeing ever so lucidly through the back walls of the building, that cheerful strip of blacktop right-angling out of town, the shining acres of the dam and two hundred miles of mountain wall brigalow cattle-plain coastal hills to a rocking tide alive with islands.

Even now that coast-dream makes my mouth water.

I could count the people in that town on ten hands.

I start to count: Stobo, Campion, Brim, Colley, Jerrold, Rider.

I get tired of this. I tire easily these days. And I follow my eyes inside Councillor Brim's office and fail to find the sea.

How can nothing be walled by nothing?

That's easy. Later, I'll tell you.

My watch has stopped.

And I remember on the instant Wafer pressing his ear into his own stopped watch trying to find the missing pulse, then deliberately not winding but heaving the thing in a glimmering arc smack into the lake where it made a circle bigger than itself. See? Wafer said.

In the bite of that mid-day heat he had made a decision against clocks.

"We're the second hands," he had said out loud. "We are the only movers. Sixty seconds to the minute equals nothing."

And that was the first time I had heard Wafer utter the word "divest".

Not possible for me now to give the exact day or even

month of Wafer's entry into Allbut for it happened when I was away at the coast and for the first year or so that he was there with his sad little attempt at reclusion, I have only confused memories from occasional holidays spent on my fading father's property of the town's initial outrage then interest then grudging acceptance. Later, the venom.

I reckon now, sprawled on my day-bed guilt, that there was the full cycle and the town wasn't really different from anyplace else except that its final actions become more redly horrible as I think about them.

Wafer was a blow-in.

Why he blew our way — and I say "our" because the town has left its itch on my skin as well — when every other karma bum was mumbling mantras through lush coast nirvanas, no one could imagine unless he was a desert father, a brutal self-purger who wanted a landscape skinned to the bone. Yet he drove in quietly one dry winter and set himself up on a piece of land on the dam-side ten miles out of town. On the east and southern sides of the little lake there were two great rock knobs, partly grassed and scrubby, and it was on the southern hill that he roosted so that on certain days, perched two hundred feet up, he could see the hill and himself on it dog-paddling in the water below.

Which was the real hill? The real man?

The real sky or its reflection?

Or the real landscape?

Allbut's a dull town. Was.

I was ripe for Wafer.

I've always been ripe for a lot of things. A silly girl, father used to call me, a bloody silly girl without a thought in her head. Which rather sounds as if I'm look-

3

ing for excuses. I don't need excuses. I was and probably always will be Miss Living Impulse of — don't ask the year. For God's sake don't ask the year.

Let me start again. I was born into the squatting class several decades back, the war over, a returned father who had achieved officer class, not because of any innate ability to lead but because he'd been to the right private school, an older brother, Jam (I've forgotten his real name) and a mother whose own father had been a South Yarra merchant of no conscience and much money. He fell off his luxury yacht in Samoa when I was five. Well, mother said between bouts of prescriptive tears, that solves the boarding-school problem for both of you. Father was rubbing his hands quietly, too. The whole property began to look up. After he had restocked the herds and built a new bunk-house for the hands, he learnt to ignore the three of us. Later, when Jam achieved manhood, father would begin to take an interest again. Too late, Father.

I was seven when I discovered how much my family bored me.

Move forward ten years.

Return to Go.

They had been sponsoring me for three terms at a southern art school. I was home for the Christmas vacation.

My boredom, I discover, had persisted into adulthood (is this normal?), so that this luncheon table with father and mother disliking each other from its baronial ends becomes the epicenter of disaster. Jam, with no vestige of his posh boarding-school adhering to his sun-scorched face, is talking with his mouth full about bulls.

Somewhere, I told myself, there is wit and gentleness and grace. I was wrong, of course, though I spent much astigmatic time in search; but then I was impatient.

My fault. The table rocked neurasthenically. Into the

backdrop of their faces, smudged out of focus, I chucked all my sour little bombs of protest that whistled round their cringing and appalled ears. I loved you. I couldn't help myself. Mother started those stale tears.

I could have, should have, been pliable. I could have been the daughter of their Sunday social page dreams and married the raw-boned son of some other grazier. I could have entered the public service the moment I finished school and vanished without trace. Or rendered my sexual misjudgements profitable with professional jobbery in the crackerjack years. My days hoot fruitily about me.

This must be the briefest of personal histories for it has taken all those yammering hours to realize the nonsense of self and if there should be trapped on the web of my greedy consciousness sharp moments of persisting stubborn pleasure taken solo, I must ignore them here for it wasn't solitariness I wanted even though solitariness had been the spring of almost any recollected delight; it was people. A long search for people. I'll put a girdle round my days in forty lines!

Advance two years. There is no talent in me, but I do have a flair. My drawings might blubber an interrogatory track across the paper but with colour I strut, canter, gallop right out of the banal. I cease being bored. Deep in colour I can forget most things, even the trumpeter husband I seem to have acquired on impulse my second year away after a mid-term lunch. I date it that way.

And after that failed, the sounds of parental "I told you so's" still echoing, a banana commune somewhere up the coast and an ancient Swede called Torben with wispy remnants of Viking beard, a piratical red scarf and wretchedly jerking legs. I am beginning to forget my husband's name.

The paint flows easily into canvases I flog to mug

tourists who scour the nearby hills looking for slum colour. I sense exploitation – is the world living off me? – and soon I am unable to see Torben for valium.

Move back to Go.

It's go, now, often and often, on the coast miscalled Sunshine of the vanishing sand, the varicosed bitumen, the high blood-pressure of high-rise.

This motel and then that. House-maiding for visitors to our endless summer, waitressing in plastic diners, mittel-Europe type tea-rooms, health bars, my eyelids turning chrome. There is Willi. And after Willi, Sam. I lose all energy. There is Jackson.

Jackson is a travelling man.

Townsville, the Isa, Darwin, Broome. "Paint," Jackson says. "Paint." As father said – how long ago was that? – a stupid girl.

Returned to Allbut, I find my parents seated over the same lunch I exploded five years before. Jam is still sputtering through lumps of rare beef. His teeth are like piano keys. Mother and father are too frail to fight.

Mother, working away daintily at a piece of potato, complains that a man has been ringing for me, collect. And ringing. His name? I demand. Jackson, she says.

My private and my public worlds are becoming confused. And by private I do not mean the escape hatch of father's hectares, the sprawling station-house. There is that, of course, in a purely physical sense, but the inner country where I keep my screwed up rag of self with its primitive wants and silent expressive yowls, has been invaded by a succession of spongers who take my talent, however minuscule, onto their tote-trays and flog it about like choc ice.

In the bowels of me, I know I'm not really much of a painter, dauber, sketcher. But then, who is? I've simply enlisted with what someone once called that great army marching towards insignificance and it seemed to me that if I were to stave off nine to five boredom what more attractive way to do it? There's that phoney cachet for a start, the untaxable quid if you're facile and the control you have over time. That's the thing — the control over seconds minutes hours, handling the *days* like a craftsman in this war against clocks.

Jackson's very name rouses my uncontrolled drybones giggle.

Mother, father, that should have warned you.

I am my own epicenter.

I am about to crumble.

Oh for five years now I have been painting the very heart of boredom and no one has recognized it: the ennui of landscapes yawning stale-breathed before the inevitability of seasons, the weltschmerz of battery people, cloned cars, the lassitude of coastal tides mumbling the same things over and over to an equally uninterested shoreline. All that clichéd wrack! My leaves droop with green tedium, city skylines collapse in exhaustion and even my abstractions of those things secrete what I can only call an interesting fatigue. Could that be why my paintings sell? There's that semi-revealed humdrummery as if the very subjects were half a-grin because they were chokka.

He says, mother continues gently, that you cannot live without him.

My long scream of rage seemed to continue days after my parents settled me into an expensive nursing home on the coast.

"We still love you, dear," mother kept saying and writing right up to the week she died. "After all, we are your parents."

Released to my cluttered room at Allbut, where now? I ask myself angrily. Where? Where?

A trip, a little soother, is arranged.

Move forward to Go.

I am bored in England France Italy Denmark Sweden and an even smaller town in Germany. Desperate, I cross the Atlantic.

I am bored in San Francisco and Los Angeles and particularly so in New Orleans. I ride a bus to New York to catch a plane home and then, on the verge, the very verge I swear, of refutation, of the discovery of interest, of the energy of under-privilege, of vigour, vigour, it is to find a telegram from Western Union asking me to return.

Mother's grave-pall is not worse than the sombre folds of Allbut which reach out across the Pacific, fogging plane and mind as I fly back.

Return to One.

I was ripe for Wafer.

Where was Wafer from, we wonder.

Rumours spun webs and town names hung on them like trapped flies. Hamburg. Basle. Copenhagen. Of course he had the right looks for any of those places, blond-grey draggle locks hauled back in a meagre ponytail, grainy white skin and the faintest memory of an accent on certain words.

The town never really discovers.

Wafer moves in his bone cage like a torch of shuttered light that startles the yokels. He manages rare but catching laughter, good nature and generosity with a capacity to remain unknown, unknowable. Sometimes he drives into town for supplies sporting what looks like a ragged ginger toga, his bare feet poking dustily below flap hems while shopkeepers roll their eyes. He is too old for this sort of caper, but he rolls his own eyes with them. He is the first to point out his strange appearance and this underscores an apparent unawareness of the tacit tapped forehead, the raised shoulders, the sideways nods. How can they cope? He smiles at children, blacks, old gummy folk. He doesn't count his change. How can they cope? How can they savage the unaware? How can the town become what it did?

I think about it now not wanting to think about it and

outside the sweating louvres of my now-town the sun flashes the morse of it back and back.

The town. Just to think of it. Hardly a town.

A cluster of thirty buildings, a blackened fringe of aboriginal humpies as far out as we can persuade them and the carcasses of seven dead cars. Metal junk rusts easy under the scrub beside the bitumen and has become part of the landscape this town cannot bear to part with.

Under the bounce of December heat.

There's a school, two-teacher, closed for summer, a shire office soon to be closed down, a police station, a store that sells canned food, frozen meat and melting ice-cream with a petrol pump by the kerb. Once a month a tanker comes here to fill it. There's a hardware store garnished with chain-saws cans of paint snake boots bolts of material hurricane lamps tanned with dust sun-downers' hats twill britches and plastic garbage bins. They have never shifted those garbage bins. There's a small haberdasher's and a one-box room that doubles as post-office and bank. We all double here. There's a leaning two-storeyed pub called The Wowser. Jesus! I ask you. I know now why mother wept, wept under the slow bombardment of sun and cicada, white-ant and dry-rot.

"Don't slam that door," the locals warn each other, heavily jokey. "The whole place will fall down."

I am going to slam that door.

There's the shell of a school of arts, a bit of architectural lah-di-dah with its verandahs and porches and carved architraves, a left-over from the days when the town was prosperous with tin mines back in the hills and travelling shows came through. Red yellow white the streamers dangle still above the stage piano where a three piece band used to whine through the numbers chalked up on a blackboard. They're still there. I see them there, saw them for years, unchanged through my childhood: Your Cheatin Heart, says the copper-plate, Spanish Eyes, South of the Boarder!

I'd cry, but for heat-dazzle.

I blink time back and read again the notice that stayed for years chalked up under the dance list: The most beautiful workmanship displayed on the figures of the dancers was the costumes. Thank you Mrs Amherst. The Allbut Concert Company Ballet.

Why has no one rubbed it out? Perhaps I am not the only one fighting clocks.

In the middle of the bitumen strip on a fenced patch of weeds and Noogoora burr is our war memorial. I know the names — there are only six — like a mnemonic for dying: Wieland, Amherst, Swan, Nehmer, Jerrold, Rider.

Across the bottom of the stone someone has scrawled in red paint: "This is what we fought for" with an arrow pointing downtown. The words and the arrow have been there a long time and no one has bothered to remove them.

All in a bracelet of stumpies.

Basle. Hamburg. Copenhagen.

Still not known.

But we know other things.

He's too friendly with the blacks. The town hates that.

He doesn't drink.

They marvel.

Someone says he's an artist, musician, writer? Is he a poof?

He is trying to create a farm on the edge of that lonely lake.

He has been seen wandering naked about his boundaries. Is he a pervert?

He has bought picks and a rock-drill and blasting material. Is he a miner?

11

Is he a God freak? Crim on the run? Illegal migrant?
Before I've been back two weeks, I discover.

In a town the size of this one – hardly a town – it is
impossible to avoid anyone.

Meeting after meeting. Sitting on memory's front
verandah I can recall the primitive trivia of this particular encounter because its consequences have tailed
me for ten years.

The vines mother had planted years before along the
rim of our house were alight with magenta coloured
bracts and honey-eaters. There's a mess of worn outdoor
furniture, a blue ashtray overflowing with stubs, three
copies of *The Cattleman's Guide* and a dying potplant. I
sit sprawled in father's lounger, happily becalmed, and
for the moment I believe in recovery, that the screen
projection of my brain pulsings would show a dull sym-
metry of light spots blinking evenly along. Torben, Willi,
Sam, Jackson – they have now the ideal quality of
observed cartooning. I can barely remember my
husband's first name. I certainly can't remember his
second.

The morning is humming. All sorts of distant sounds,
muted and made respectable, drift in to me where I play
valetudinarian, conscious of Tottie Stamp, our for ever
cook, crashing pans in the kitchen over baking smells;
somewhere a toilet flushes, a radio is switched on.
Without bothering to look up I hear Jam riding back into
the home paddock, sense him tethering his horse by the
verandah steps, follow his boyish boundings toward
elevenses and pushing aside some speculative vinery I
observe a stranger walking along our drive, not tentatively as a stranger might, but squarely marking the
size and qualities of trees, looking right and left with the

12

concentration of confidence. He is naked, except for a pair of bathing trunks.

It is Wafer, heard of but not yet met. Jam looks disapproving but unsurprised.

His van, Wafer tells us, has bogged in a creek a mile back. Could we pull him out? We could, Jam says, observing the draggle locks, and child-look in the eye. Jam is uncomfortable, anxious to be away again but waits for Tottie's scones impatiently, gulping and munching when they arrive as if he wants to appall us all. No tea, thank you, Wafer says. Just water. Jam snorts with disgust. He gets up, says will you see to it, sis − the old boy is having trouble with a couple of steers − and rides off.

Confronted. Confronting.

There is no hurry for the van. A bit of scone butter has dropped and melted between his toes. I am determined he will talk to me.

Wafer is a bomb age baby.

He's earlier than that.

My daddy, Wafer remembered, had given farm-life away, found himself a copy boy's job in Sydney, graduated to a reporter's desk, staggered through a course in politics and insinuated himself by sheer gall as well as talent into the department of foreign affairs. He became a press attache at the High Commission in London and during a summer walking tour in Scandinavia met and married on the spot a Swedish girl who was pretending to paint seascapes at Skagen. Oh the summertime artists, Wafer said to me. And the light, the purity of tone that hints at the naive intentions of all those Sunday painters in the summer cottages along the sandhills. I was conceived, he said, behind the point where two seas meet.

He was born, I discover, to Czechoslovakian rumbles, weaned during the Jewish purges and about to be tucked into a bottom bunk on a liner leaving for Australia via

13

the Cape just as Churchill discovered rhetoric. The day before the boat sailed his mother took him back to London, despite the blitz, to say goodbye to his father. She was waving across the street at him, tugging at her little boy to cross, when he saw his father disintegrate before his eyes.

Of course, he said mildly, sipping his water, we should never have taken the risk.

When the bomb dropped on Hiroshima an egg-eyed Wafer could barely be hauled from the radio as if he had some terrible intimacy with all the connotations of disaster. Furtively he read reports of skins shed like coats, like ragged streamers of shirt, of revolting burns, his child face looking as if it heard down the ocean currents the dying screams beneath the mushroom cloud. News pictures, press reports, stories of bomb-seeded coups became the terrifying pornography he coddled in secret right through his acne years in a cave-like region of blue funk. Despite the toted placebo everyone lipped — "They'll never use it!" — he twitched his nervous way through boarding-school, half a philosophy course, left-wing politicizing, public service serfdom and odd-jobbing as a union functionary until finally, his late thirties crowding him, he was surrounded, he discovered, by symphonies of nuclear reactors and afraid.

Europe on nothing a year, he said. The Australian cliché, he said. Squatting with the summer troops of back-packers in the town squares of Hamburg, Amsterdam, Stockholm, he swapped his ideal neurosis, legs out-stretched in what passed for summer, with the fears of young Germans, Cockneys, Frenchmen, Danes, Americans. It was the Americans, he said, who scared him home.

Back to his mother's three room Clontarf flat and her teaching pension. He had rubbed Harbour blue out of his Europe-greyed eyes while his mother asked doubt-fully; "And what will you do now?"

"I'm looking for the perfect bomb shelter," he told her.

"Don't be like that, dear," his mother said. "I was hoping you'd got over all that."

"I was hoping," he had said, hoping, "that you might be different from the rest of this blinkered world. After all," he added not deliberately cruel, "you know."

His parting with her was brief and emotionally un-finished as if some predicate of family living were left hanging in the air.

"But where?"

"This country," he explained, "is the perfect bomb shelter. That's achieved at least. And then the shelter within the shelter."

"But there's no shelter for the mind," his mother said. Nor was she deliberately cruel when she said, "You know."

Well, that remark is the tears of things, uttered bleakly in our continental funkerama, our desert saucer where the towns have been chucked about like a losing toss of dice on a vast baize of dead felt. Hundreds of these towns.

As he searched, he odd-jobbed, relaxed with the ironically flat ramparts of the land about him, moving easy, shoving his second-hand campervan north and west through sheep wheat oranges pineapples bananas cattle until somewhere in the top of the country the nothingness of the landscape became delight as he found a particular scrambling of the dice, a lake, some sky-nudging knobs of hill as if they had been waiting all those years just for him.

The scones are finished. The water has been drunk. We are left facing each other with something? nothing? to say.

"You're not really afraid," I suggest, stupidly incredulous in the perfection of the day, blue blinding taut, tacitly offering as support all the mundane steadiers about us — kitchen sounds, the shortening shadows, the homely barking of the dogs. He only smiled, so I got up, brought the truck around with its tow ropes and went down the road to his bogged car. I think I must be unused to simplicity, to honesty.

It was only when he turned from the window of his van to thank me that he answered my question.

"Once," he said. "Now it's simply something I have to do."

This is a clean and decent town. How can I describe the temper of it?

There were three funerals the first week I was home.

"Poor – um – soul!" this and that one commented as Archie Wetters was lowered in his town-subscribed pine box into the baked earth of Allbut cemetery. Storm heads dangled over the map as I changed from foot to aching foot with the rest of the waiting townsfolk, listening to the minister who had been brought fifty miles from the next township having trouble when it came to the bon voyage prayers.

"Our beloved – um – sister in Christ," he finally managed with chilling hesitation that made our little crowd drop its eyes, "Archie Wetters," for it was discovered after Archie's death – a riotous heart attack in the front bar of the Wowser – that he was a woman.

Archie had been living alone in a flea-box on the edge of town for the last twenty years and was one of our characters. How old when he died? we asked. People guessed seventy. Guessed eighty. There he went shambling down the main street in the last few years shoving an old pram to wheel his groceries, his money tied up in the corner of a dirty handkerchief, a string of dogs sniffing lovingly at his bare heels.

The town was stunned.

Arch had been a boundary rider for years before he came to us, working on one of the Gulf stations, and had jockeyed at the picnic race meetings for miles around. He was still riding when he settled here. Everyone had struggled to recall the wind-skimmed outline of his buttercup silks and could recall very little. Once, when I was ten or eleven, I had seen him ride a winner and I had watched the wiry little fellow leading his mount back to the rub-down enclosure crazily grinning because he had beaten two of the best riders in the area. I remember, not so much because of Arch, but because the day was luminous, drenched in eucalyptus and noisy with clean cold sounds of the creek beside the course so that I was filled with a tenacious delight that ran through my body like love.

I dropped my eyes to the hole where Arch had vanished and watched the minister scatter ritual dust. "Poor old bugger," someone said behind me. And someone else said, "He wasn't a bad old sod. Not when you consider he was a woman."

Wind kept scribbling the dust about, altering, undoing his legend.

I looked sideways at my father who was gummed to his ceremonial tie like the rest of the townsmen. His thumbs kept tugging at his collar, easing his neck, and the collar was already rimmed with red dust and sweat. Wearing the rags, the conventional rags, I thought ironically, vulgarly, turning a euphemism I'd picked up from Jam and always hated, straight back to its source. At that very moment I was conscious of a rush of sisterhood for Arch, dear old Arch, deaf now to the our father which art and remembering his blood-shot eyes bright with something (I knew now what it was) as he shuffled up the dusty street to the pub. Couldn't really think of him hallowed be his name as she, those bandy jockey's legs, the lace of grey curls, the face doubly lined oh ever so well lived in his kingdom come.

"Old Arch is a moph," the kids used to say, repeating their dads' summations. "A moph."

"What's a moph, father?" I had asked that night at tea. "It's two bob each way," father said. "Pass the beans." Jam had rolled about.

"Tell me," I shouted. "Tell me." Hating their knowledge, their superior sly smiles.

One afternoon when I was twelve and knew Archie was up town, I had sneaked into his shack on a dare.

But there was nothing there, really, under the frenzied yapping of chained dogs: bits of cooking stuff, letters, papers and an odd jumble of books. (Books were enough to label him queer in a town like Allbut.) Strange books, they were: poetry, religion. A huge tome called *The Golden Bough* whose me-riffled pages were crammed with difficulties that prickled now, fifteen years on, as I hear the fragments of amens tossed all round the grave like more of the ritual dust. "When he lies down," one of my classmates had argued about Archie's sex, "his stomach stays up. He's got to be a woman." Clever Arch, I was saying to myself, as father and Jam nudged me along with the trail of mourners to the cemetery gates. Clever lucky Arch.

I'd known about Arch since that afternoon in the shack.

All those inscriptions, the ink brownly stating "To Clancy with love from Mum and Dad", "Dearest Clementine, for her twelfth birthday", "To Clancy from her loving Aunt Bo". But I never said.

"What you find out?" the other kids pestered me under the pepper trees next day. Oh there was my first good deed.

"Nothing," I lied. I was practising too the protective

veneers of womanhood had I known. "Not a thing. Just some old cups and things and a stock whip. Nothing."

I tried not to think but mortality grumbled in my ear wringing me out as I saw beneath my slanted eyelids hung with crystals of heat or tears the whole doomed pack of us trailing back to the parked cars as if we were imperishable. The permitted three score and ten.

Scratchy with this inflammation I roughly multiplied father's projected span by days and whispered softly,

"Do you realize you only have two thousand three hundred days left, give or take a few."

"Stop your nonsense," father said, not really hearing. "Stop it at once." He had already begun removing his tie.

It seems a lot shorter that way, doesn't it, counting in days? Months are soul-stopping. I'm glad I didn't say "father, you have only ninety-six months." Even if you absorb the whole of the biblical life-span and express it in weeks, the brevity is stunning. It must be the effect of inflation.

They buried Tommy Wildapple two days later; not that I went to the funeral for it was held out at the mission station fifty miles west; and if I tell you about that funeral as well, it's partly to explain the nature of our town and its particular humour that summer. Trouble rose and broke like a blister.

Tommy Wildapple's sister, Rosie Wonga, his only living next-of-kin, was notified of her brother's death in the hospital at Mainchance. She and her twelve year old son started off for Mainchance from Allbut with their new funeral clothes packed in a plastic case, setting out to walk the ten miles or so to the branch-line. But it was Wafer who picked them up and gave them a lift. The town, fresh from burying old Arch and already in shock, was critical. "Fair enough if they stink out his car," they said. But even after the lift things went wrong. The Mainchance train broke down twice and by the time

20

Rosie arrived at the hospital, they had boxed Tommy up, and were on the point of shipping him back down the line for burial at the Mission.

"How come you don't bury him here?" Rosie asked. "I come a long way for this, eh? You got a big cemetery here."

They told her he had wanted to go back.

"When you dead you dead," Rosie said. "I done this trip for nothun then. What he die of? Can I see him?"

"Can't see him now," they told her. "You got here too late.'

Rosie began to cry.

"What he die of?" she asked between snuffles.

Leprosy, they told her.

"Get away!" Rosie shouted. "You're lying. He was cured of that long time back. Doctor told him he was cured. I seen him four maybe five years back. He don't have no leprosy then. He have leprosy why he still workun out on them big cattle places, eh? He have heart attack more like. He get thrown maybe. Kicked by horse. Don't have no leprosy no more."

Her wails filled the reception room and the office and the staff became impatient with her.

"I don't have no more money to go out the Mission," she said. "All that way."

Across the bent heads of Rosie and her son, the matron and nurse at the desk exchanged glances.

"You can ride out in the hearse, I suppose. Would you do that?"

Rosie nodded.

"Then someone at the Mission's sure to give you a lift back to Allbut. It's not that far."

"Both of us?" Rosie asked. "Billy too?"

The hearse took the back road, completing the circle-sweep that Rosie was condemned to, but thirty miles out of Allbut Mission, a police car caught up with the

21

hearse, forced it to the side of the road in explosions of bull-dust and pulled up just ahead of it. Sergeant Cropper, massive with authority, ordered Rosie and her boy out.

"Bring your bag, Nellie," he said.

Rosie took her bag out of the back and put it down on the dried grass by the roadside. It didn't weigh very much. Sergeant Cropper leaned in through the window of the hearse presenting great buttocks and stretched tight thighs to the afternoon sun. Rosie could not hear what he said but in a moment he straightened up, the hearse engine grunted and the long black car began to pull away.

"What you doing?" Rosie asked.

"Get your clothes off, Nellie," the copper ordered. "His too."

He was a meaty man whose eyes seemed to have vanished behind sun-glare.

Rosie began to shake. "I'm not gettun no clothes off, mister. You can't make me do that."

The sergeant began to roll a cigarette. He wasn't in any hurry.

"Quarantine, Nellie. You know that word, eh? You and sonny-Jim here can't go joy-riding with a corpse that's leprous, can you? Not even you, eh? All this stuff has to be burned." He had stopped smiling and listened to Rosie cry for a minute before he lit up.

"Not me bag," she said. "Not all me new stuff. All me new stuff."

Sergeant Cropper cupped his hand about his cigarette and lit it. He inhaled and exhaled then in a huge comic sigh.

"Okay, Nellie," he said. "Cut out the sob stuff please. I told you and I'm telling you again and I'm not going to wait all day. Get your clothes off and the kid's and give us that bag over there."

There was a small tussle.

"Now," Sergeant Cropper said. "Now your clothes."

Rosie and her son stood naked in the heat.

The copper barely glanced at them.

"Pick all that stuff up. Pick it up!"

Rosie and her boy gathered up the bag, the garments.

"Now," Sergeant Cropper ordered, "take them through into that paddock, see? Make a heap, all nice and tidy, eh?"

He went back to his car and took a jerrycan of petrol from the boot, walked over to the little pile of clothing and poured petrol on it.

"Okay," he said. "Stand back now."

He tossed a lighted match onto the clothes, stepping back smartly from the whump. For a few minutes the fire blazed viciously and the suitcase melted like cheese. Cropper kicked the glinting ashes about with his boot.

Behind him Rosie let out a long terrible wail.

"Shut up, Nellie," he said over his shoulder. "We're nice and clean now."

"What we do, eh?" she kept asking. Her son rubbed a snotty nose. "What we do?"

"Dunno what you're gunna do, Nellie," Cropper said with heavy good nature. He grinned not quite normally. "But I'm going back to Allbut. There'll be a car out to pick you up."

"Tommy's funeral!" Rosie shouted. She was sitting huddled in the dirt by the side of the road, covering herself with her skinny arms. Billy squatted beside her, too scared to yowl. "I'll miss the funeral. I'm gunna miss Tommy's funeral."

"You couldn't have gone on in that hearse, Nellie," the sergeant said. He ground out the stub of his cigarette. "It's against regulations. And I can't go driving out there with you like that, now can I? Eden-naked, you might say. Christ! What would people say! But you go on in

23

that hearse, Nellie, and we might have had to burn you too."

He didn't smile. He took one last grind at the smouldering heap and rolled back to his car.

By the time someone drove out from the Mission to pick them up, it was too late for the funeral. Tommy had been buried and she could only stand by the freshly dug grave and squeeze her son's hand.

"Them white barstids," she kept crying between snuffles. "Them white barstids."

And again, like some prismatic smiling in the sulky landscape, it was Wafer who drove out to the mission to fetch them back to the elemental tinscape of their Allbut humpy. It was Wafer who fitted them up with some new clothes.

I think that was the start of it then, for Sergeant Cropper stopped Wafer as he drove Rosie and her boy back into town and booked him for careless driving.

Wafer had a theory that the chemical structure of places acted like sensitized paper which absorbed not only the bodily presence but also the emotional patterns of voice and eyes, the abstract emotions doled out by tears or smiles and that the place kept projecting these images onto further sensitized material that was himself.

Nothing new about that, I suppose, but his quiet delivery lent validity. For there was no flux in time, he was convinced — and convinced me for our impermanent summer — accepting seasons, months, days, as all seasons, months, days, so that the radiance of any blossomed morning on a Thursday, say, was the same when his body marked Friday. Still Thursday, still Thursday, he grieved or exulted, the Thursday of Magna Carta, Borodino, the Bay of Pigs and Hiroshima, always Hiroshima, shuddering under its deadly corolla while he and a billion saved others walked on to the death-pause he saw as a kind of heli-pad stop.

But still Thursday.

He had begun to create his fastness two years ago.

On a Thursday. He tells me that and I laugh. Would I care to see it? Soon, I say. Soon. We have run into each other again at the store and drip groceries and sweat. Town eyes observe with interest as we sag towards each other in the heat. There are five drinkers slumped above their life-force on the pub verandah, Mrs Councillor Brim tweaking the ghastly frocks of the dummies in her haberdashery window, Sergeant Cropper bullying a cigarette in his parked police car and Emmeline Colley tripping her thirteen, fourteen years down the steps of the Post Office into the bike-propped adoration of Timothy Rider.

We should be a nice little town, a clean and decent place, for the houses are filled with ordinary folk who eat cooked breakfasts, listen to the six o'clock news, de-tick their dogs and go to sleep in front of the television.

Three days go by. Father crashes each evening before a commercial channel that has only recently achieved transmission to Allbut and is supposed to be enlarging our vision of the world. Every five minutes he takes communion from an American Colonel and a chain of fast food take-aways. I can no longer bear to watch. I have sat fascinated, too, through the esperanto of telly in Europe and America and that old sense of belonging to a tenth-rate culture has engulfed me as if Cro-Magnon man took a wrong turning somewhere. "Do you watch 'Dallas'?" my hosts in Denmark shyly asked and were gently hurt by my amusement. "It's like the Mass in Latin," I replied. Their eyes registered non-comprehension.

"The Church used to argue for the use of Latin that it gave you a sense of familiarity in any part of the world."

"Oh." They look offended. "Oh."

It's amusing, isn't it, to know that "Dallas", or the "The Incredible Hulk" or "Hawaii Five-0" have taken the place of the Tridentine Mass.

Out here, of course, the emphasis is on manly games. I say to father one Friday night with the old box roaring away, "Is there only a choice between crotch sniffers and cricketers with menstruation envy? Those red streaked groins!"

"Jesus, Gabby," Jam says. "You're sick." He turns the volume up.

I brood in my room and all next day I sketch telly viewers hobbled by their cathode ray tubes, their glazed faces upturned for the fast food manna that drops like noisy rain from heaven. If I allow my anger to seed, there will be no saving me.

On the next day I drive out to the dam.

It is early and the new upspringing of burr about the monument, the dead cars, the strip of blacktop still glisten with dew. I give a lift to Rosie Wonga trudging home to her shanty. She smells of sweat and onions and can hardly speak for shyness. My heart receives a savage charge as it did when I was very young and I start to sing, catching the shy corner of Rosie's puzzled smile. Goodbye Rosie. Waves to the cooboos. Goodbye kids. Round the spur now and the excitement speeds me rocking along the dam road, the rock humps coming into view as I reach the crest and then the dam spread out in its shining acres as I take a side-track winding along the water rim.

Wafer's few acres are obscenely green. There are fruit trees, still very young, and a vegetable patch and there is an absurd eyrie perched atop the rock, a brief sparkle on an iron roof to the side of the next hill fold and a double decker bus paddling at the lake edge five hundred yards away.

Why this choking sense of expectation?

I stop the car, gulp in summer heat and step out.

Wafer is walking slowly, naked through the morning, down the track to meet me.

It had taken him a year to excavate and line to his manic satisfaction a dug-out small enough (I look at his limpid eyes! He doesn't appear mad. Certainly no madder than I.) and large enough for his capability and his needs. The concrete block walls of his underground womb wrap him in a deadening content and squatting on his shelter floor, the crazy Job, he would visualize the amniotic quality of future living among his canned food stacks, his water barrel, his trim little cess pit.

And above the shelter rises the other house the world can see, an airy cage of verandah and curious clouds.

"But the world is the ultimate bomb," I say, leaning against his shaky railing. "Its shape. Its storehouses. Its spinning velocity. We are living on the bomb."

He looked curiously at me for a moment as if what I said surprised him. I could see he was shaken.

"Of course." He pretended absorption in the view. "Oh of course."

I am ashamed of my remark, the rawness of it. His half-turned neck seems to quiver. There is a patch of unhealed sunburn on one knobby shoulder. His genitals − I don't really like to look − appear to have shrunk.

"Excuse me," he says.

I am left on the verandah while he rummages for shorts, brooding over shelters I have known: a pre-bomb party in Florida in an après-bomb shelter, the whole caboodle a plastic and shag-pile farce of discreet lighting, emergency generators, chemical toilets and a bar with twelve months' supply of bourbon; a kitsch survival pit in upstate New York with gnomes and five-hundred cans of soup for a post-bomb-survival-fest; a hippy dugout in southern California with nothing but records and books and an old wind-up gramophone. "There'll be hash," they told me, "stacked later. Lady, we'll go out smiling, smiling." And there were those I read about, gun-fierce land-holders in the Rockies who were determined to hold their caves against survivors. And appearing, coyly at first and then with open money concern, the advertisement for the "underground home with two feet thick walls, as smart for pre-bomb living as for later. Practical, too," the ads went on. "What a play house for the kids on rainy days! Send them below when you have guests for dinner! They'll think it a wow!"

Wafer re-appears, modest in tee shirt and shorts, and I am aware of the oddity of him, as if he were one red-veined eyeball confronting naked dawn upon dawn miles off the karma tracks.

"Come in," he says, not meeting my amused mouth which had been, I swear, smiling at American hustling.

But we were already in, for there are merely the outlines of walls to the sides and rear. There is only one room as if he needs the encapsulation of a space he can administer at a glance and he did not have to explain to me, not to me, his need to examine the quality of smallness where every spider web, gecko dropping, patterned an exquisite communion bread. He must have cooked somewhere but I was not conscious of anything except posters and books and one shadowy lump of gemstone resting beneath a cardboard notice he had tacked to the wall.

The sign said "divest".

The gemstone mocked the sign.

Later I discovered that once each day the sun struck the stone to muezzin life and something blazed inside for a moment, speaking its name.

"Look up," Wafer tells me, grinning now.

Above me, writ huge, "sealing".

And to my stunned right, "whorl".

I think about it.

"You've missed one," I say to the precious bastard. "Flaw".

He's simply one of those, I think sulkily, who can tote his overnight bag of crap metaphysics through whatever landscape he's in.

29

"You're mocking me, of course."

"No," I lie. "No."

But he grins more widely as if he's had a lot of mocking and says, "But they're a joke."

And now he's lying.

I must make it clear from the start that Wafer wasn't really a liar. Let's say he had had to protect himself from a lot of jocular bastardry throughout his life and if at forty-plus — he looked older sometimes with that tired and strained face — the world made him nervous, I do understand that, oh I understand.

I wanted to know who lived beneath house glint, under bus.

He talked as if he hadn't heard. This was a disused school-house he explains, moved across, the usable pieces, bit by bit. In the slack of afternoons he had begun to become increasingly attuned to the building's origins: child smell, lunchbox scents of bread and bananas, pencil-shavings, erasers. Who lives in the bus? Ignored. And later, whisperings, giggles and the airy substance of nudges, carefully positioned trip-legs, bare feet and cries from a vanished school-yard each day between noon and one. Or the house? The house I can just see?

He really believed his own words and even now, so long after, I can see Wafer's long anxious face half a-smile with the nerve, the sheer nerve, of what he was saying, inspecting me for the dreaded laugh.

I didn't laugh.

"You haven't heard a word," he accused. "Not a word."

"All of them. I heard all of them." I knew my next remark must be careful. "You're so cut off here, you're peopling the place. You need more people."

"That's exactly what I don't need." A quick flush on each cheek-bone. "Colley lives over there in the house with his daughter. They haven't been there long. A few

30

months. A fellow called Moon has the bus. He came a year ago and we see all we need of each other. I'm not a recluse, not a genuine recluse, but I do simply want to be. Just to be. Can you understand that?"

"And you never get bored?"

"Bored? Are you serious?"

"I wish I weren't."

How could I explain all the ingredients of disillusion that had badgered me into retreat: the last quack nursing home, the car salesman of a psychiatrist who explained my little misdemeanours, my incursions into shop-lifting, motel-scrounging, as all part of the scars left by over-strict teachers, over-indulgent teachers, bed-wetting (I have never wet the bed), early irregular periods, parental indulgence, parental discipline, sibling envy, a disastrous first marriage (do you achieve orgasm?), sexual immaturity and now we'll give her a rigorous course of stelazine, valium, amytal. I'm bored, I shout into his twenty-eight chalk-white teeth. Bored bored bored. Nurse, he says, Miss Jerrold is upset. Nurse. His island-tanned suavity is unmoved even when I hit out at him. That's right, my dear. That's right. Hit. You must not repress. But punished later with a long-term long-sleep needle.

I could begin to snivel. I am still not well. That gives Wafer reassurance, my working mouth, and something to do. There's some kind of drink at my elbow. His anxious face. The flick of a finger touch. This is too absurd.

I shake my head as if tears were rain-water.

"There isn't much time for boredom," he says. "We don't have enough time in the survival race."

"I paint it."

"Paint what?"

"Boredom. All aspects of, ever since I can remember."

"But how? So boredom's interesting, then?"

I'll show him some time, some time when I can gauge the responsibility of his reply.

Like Wafer, I can't bear to be laughed at.

I am becalmed.

It is two weeks until Christmas.

It is a week, after days of seeing, since I have seen Wafer.

I brood. I watch a nervous rash on my hands mature and die. Like my heart, I think indulgently. Father asks me to help with the accounts. Jam is too busy. Well, that's a laugh, but I do, and spend ten sneezing hours in the store-room.

I think about Wafer. I am not a sentimentalist but I think about Wafer because he is gentle, because he is uninterested in me and I confess I want his interest, and because he is afraid. And there are two others I think about as well, two who are necessary to the horribleness of what our little town did.

There is Emmeline Colley, forever tripping lightly and with punctilious grace down the Post Office steps to Timothy Rider propping his adoration against an old two-wheeler. They are both home from boarding-school and though they have known each other for the last few months, briefly, it is only now they appear to have met.

And there is Moon.

I can tell you about Moon now, though what I tell was not all known then.

Moon lives beneath his occasional flags of washing strung from the double-decker bus on the allotment next to Wafer's. For a year he has been a casual odd-jobber around the town, affects miner's blue, picks about the hills with fossicker's gear and moves like a panther, his body taut under some slumbering tension that goes with a nervous and desperate temper. He drinks at the Wowser and he talks at the Wowser and Jam listens to him Friday nights when, loosened up by grog, he breaks his vow of silence and boasts of things none of us should know.

Jam tells me Moon was born in Louisiana to an Australian girl who'd married an American serviceman towards the end of the war. Wafer tells me that's a lie, that the Yankee accent is a fake. What do I believe?

Father roars that he's a draft dodger from New Zealand.

It's not always true that truth lies somewhere in the middle. Let's go with the drunken Odyssey Jam has pieced together.

Go back to Louisiana.

When he was fifteen, Moon tells Jam who tells me, his pappy died from a heart attack while shouting at a nigra who sassed him over the impoverished filling in a poboy sandwich. Moon ran away fast from the truckies' caff his mammy ran when, quick as a flash, his mammy went and married a too-dark river man who spoke mongrel French and worked the tourist boats, ran and spent three hot desperate pounding months with the whores of Basin Street and in the jazz cellars along Bourbon. He ended up riding the bus north to New York where he pulled drinks in a West Side bar until the draft caught up with him three years later and he found himself at nineteen in a combat unit in Vietnam with a licence to kill.

He's always been a loner, Jam says, with a trigger-quick temper. In village ambushes, as if swayed by some extravagant rage, he wrecked three-stripe carnage that even sickened his C.O. The awful thrill of it. (Jam's awful thrill as he tells me!) Recreation leave in Sydney found him slumbrously oppressed in bars around the Cross, trying, as he eyed the September crowds along Macleay Street to blot out the brown fleeting shapes of women and children suddenly stilled. Was there to be no end to it? He found himself longing for the line-up of pie wedges under glass, his mammy chiacking the teamsters. He began to take drugs. They were easy enough to get in Saigon; and when the States pulled out of Vietnam ("Leaving all their goddam garbage," quotes Jam) he went back to Louisiana, bony and ill, to find his mammy involved with yet a newer husband and a pair of squawling kids he couldn't believe to be his half-sisters.

Move on two squares. Three. A banana boat service from Galveston through the Caribbean, taking the run on his own, finally, through the sharky blues of the Gulf, nosing in and out of broken down ports along the Venezuelan and Brazilian coasts. The drugs caught up with him and yellow fever and he ended up in a run-down brothel on the fringes of Belem raging at the world.

When he took his first trembling steps into Rua Gaspar Viana where the sunshine lay like a stinking paste all along the waterfront, he felt as new as an alligator cracking out of its egg. Bougainvillea made elaborate fires around La Casa de las Pequeñas Muertes so that he had to shade his eyes as if the world had stopped. As it had.

In The House of the Little Deaths a Spanish Indian girl who had looked after him from the night he lost consciousness in her bed told him of a client who was running tourist parties of gawping Americanos up-river. During his fever he had lost his job on the trading boat and he was weary, anyway, of the currents of the Gulf. Soledad had pushed the two hundred cruzeiros he gave her into a box before a statue of the Virgin and watched him as he began to take off his clothes.

"Why are you telling me this?" he had asked, because he was used to indifference.

Soledad had stroked the wall on each side of her as if this total little world she had come to know were a love-object in which she was transfixed. The straw-coloured walls caught soft rags of sun through leaves outside the opened casement and beyond that, only for a minute, there were bells and a man singing.

(Could Jam have told me all this, all these minutiae which now I add with the merest flick of brush-tip? I want you to listen to this story. I want. I dab light everywhere I feel I might illuminate. Jam's a plain young man, after all, part of his horse I could say, with a hey whinny whinny, and what he tells me I re-translate. Where's the lie in it? It could be as father said — trans-Tasman dole-bludger. I like it like this.)

"You need the money," she had said.

"To come back and spend on you?"

"The fever didn't reach your teeth," she said.

Put Moon there, put him there, naked and shivering between the little table with its primitive medicines and the bed.

"I'll file my teeth," he had offered which was his version of apology.

She had laughed then. "It could be as you first thought." She paused. "But it is not. This time we will do it for each other." And she began removing her clothing also with brief assertive glances that foxed his weakened body.

So he could only nuzzle her. His brutality lay like cut grass.

"Pray," he whispered into her sweating body, "pray to all the patron saints of the little death."

I am beginning to paint again. I am painting Carib rivers

I have never seen. I paint Moon into jungle landscapes like a Rousseau tiger.

Trollope, the Englishman who owned the clapped-out diesel river-boat was too tired to care about the leaking ice-box, the blistered paint-work, the permanent stutter in the motor. I paint Trollope complete with grog blossom and his own clapped-out heart. In my version, his eyes are small. "It's pretty straight-forward," he says, "so long as you don't poach on the big boys' passengers. We aim at the intimate trip." There's glare on the water round the wharves. "We split it down the middle."

Moon stuck it for six months — kids doing the trip on a shoe-string, out of towners looking for budget colour: two days up river, an over-night stop at an Indian village with a cockroach filled *pensão* and a reggae band. Two days back.

On the last trip he made, his deck-hand, a half-caste of pervasive lewdness, attempted to force the wife of one of the tourists. He had decoyed her into a dank clearing not far from their river lunch-camp and among the still unrotted coke cans and plastic wraps of previous trysts he was, despite her muffled cries, about to drown in her when Moon came looking. Unable to tell whether the cries were of pleasure or outrage, he shot the half-breed straight through the back of the head.

The wife, reacting properly after the initial shock of interrupted coitus as her husband came crashing down the track, spent her sobbing between two sets of shoulders. I paint Moon's puritanism wincing away. Both the husband and Moon decided it was better to say nothing about the matter and later they dropped the body, weighted with four demi-johns of cheap wine, into a section of the river farther upstream.

Too late for regrets.

The trigger reaction could breed years of grieving.

Re-entrance somewhere on the east coast of Africa

where he found himself a job with a safari group working the tourist racket without a permit.

There must have been some scent now in his skin that repelled without reason, for the bearers avoided him as if they could smell the sharp powder of that other death in that other country.

They rolled chocolate eyes.

They went sullen.

He bullied and they obeyed minimally.

All in this circle perfumed by decay.

But what was there except a youngish man still eroded by fever, decent enough, bone-thin, silent, who worked automatically as if his mind were concentrated on some inaccessible true north — not there, not yet.

Taking two seedy Germans for a ten day run after buffalo, an argument developed with the bearers as early as the second day out. Moon was trimming bush poles for the tents when unexpectedly one of the bearers sprang straight at him, hands curved into claws. Moon caught the movement from the side of one sad eye, half-straightened and in one continuing massive sweep of his bush knife removed the man's hands.

As he wiped the blade clean, the terrible desolation that he had been keeping at bay since Brazil surged in and not even the quick rationalization, the urgently grasped at defence, could damp down the guilt that always followed anger.

He shouldered his personal pack and gun and walked away, slipping quietly off-stage until he made his re-entrance in Sydney, thinner, tauter and silent now for longer and longer periods.

He went on acid trips. Was picked up and dumped in a dry-out centre and then, later, his head frail but lucid, moved slowly north along the New South Wales coast, working at a boat-building yard for a while, picking fruit, packing at a north coast cannery.

He bought himself a campervan and went west to fossick in the opal fields, a slow drifter curving ever north until the natural arc of his journey brought him at last into the scrubby hills beside the lake where he wrestled with memories of Soledad and La Casa de las Pequeñas Muertes and two clearings that refused to be over-grown.

How do I know all this?

There was what Jam told me and rumours and half-truths from dodgier characters in town, the gossipy intrusions of Doss Campion who pulled pints at the Wowser, the threads spun out painfully one mothy evening to Wafer − all stories grown rampant, sprouting tendrils until they covered whole structures, blunting original lines, disguising shape before the support collapsed.

Perhaps none of it was true. I choose to believe even if it is the half-heard doubled in drunken repetition.

None of us really knew. We only picked at the edges of these stories in long bush evenings after tea, scrub-crowded, the sole colonizers of planet earth, cradling our tea-cups, sprawling our legs before the welding cosiness of another's disasters and the glowing warmth given out by the "thank God I am not as one of these".

"As I said last week," father was saying smugly and moving a bishop (the television had broken down), "our history should stave off boredom and a man's history is much like that of his country's − true or false really makes no difference. It's not an exact science − check − is it? It's a compound of rumour, fact and variables like the state of the weather, Napoleon's piles, Gladstone's wife turning bitchy at her periods − all of that stuff. You can't hope to − I wouldn't move there, if I were you −

38

know it all, let alone understand it. Check-mate, I think. You can only examine the perimeters of your own involvement. That is enough. Another game?"

Ungraciously I say I might as well.

Father keeps his eyes on the board as I move my knight's pawn.

"This country," father says. "This country." He begins to laugh. (It seems strange to be talking to father — he seems to take more interest now in Jam and me than he ever did when we were younger, and while I should be pleased, my pleasure is disrupted by the fact that it is a surprise to me he has ideas about anything but cattle.)

"What about it," I say. "Go on."

"Well," he says, dangling a pawn over the board, "well, all Australia has done for two centuries — you know that old joke about rape? — is lie back and think of England. No. I'm not quite right there. Now she thinks of the States, Japan and France as well. Even West Germany. All that stuff up north of us went to a German industrialist last June before you came back. She's a regular scrubber of a country, eh? Not even a good tart. Does it with anyone anywhere any time — and doesn't get paid. No respect, Jam," he said turning to my radio-twiddling brother, "no respect, not even the sort you give to tarts, unless you get paid. This country's like a dame with hot pants — give give give to any takers. You can't move your rook there, Gabby — I speak of course of her economic ploys, not the sexual habits of her countrywomen."

"You haven't answered my question."

"Haven't I? Well, what was it?"

"Why has Cropper such a down on Wafer?"

"Chemical perhaps," father says. "I don't know. Probably can't bear seeing someone in that age-group non-conforming. A country of myth-fits. Hey, that's not really bad, is it? Myth-fits. I like that."

I take his queen's bishop as the first electric storm of the wet cuts the skies open but the game is left unfinished and we go on to the verandah to watch lightning dazzle dark to day, play in sheets of white ahead of the rocking thunder and the sharp rain that tears across our iron roofs in arpeggios of water which brings with it the sweet smell of settling dust.

It rains steadily, solidly, all through the night.

Wafer, the heavens are howling on someone's behalf. Mine? Yours?

I am not, I insist, not in love.

It's remarkable how you can see a person on and off for years and not see them. Not really see. But Wafer's strolling naked into the first fortnight of our knowing disturbed me thoroughly although I had long grown used to the idea of bare flesh from life classes, hippie communes and the surfing heavens. There were porno magazines, too, Jam kept in his underwear drawer. But paper cannot reproduce the faint half-flush etc that dies along the limbs of near stranger and for a while Wafer's brown and rosy lights colour my waking hours.

It is one week until Christmas.

I drive out to the dam in the aftermath of thunder and rain.

The lake flashes messages like a spy-glass.

There are other people on Wafer's frail verandah staring at the view. There is Mr Colley and his daughter Emmeline. There is Timothy Rider. Below, there is the vanishing back of a sullen Moon.

Emmeline Colley. Emmeline Colley. She is an almost pretty wistful child of thirteen with a smiling dad who is eager to please. We all drink coffee in the ten o'clock light and I observe Wafer watching Emmeline and Timothy Rider watching Wafer watching Emmeline and Mr Colley watching me watching all of them. Timothy Rider is the school-master's boy. He is a bright-faced

41

good-looking sixteen year old home from boarding school in an ideal conjunction with Emmie.

Irrationally I wish them together. I wish nothing to obstruct the interest that I have that Wafer might perhaps show interest in me.

Do I never learn?

Colley is naggingly working at Wafer's obsession. He throws B52s and neutron bombs into the conversation; he talks about the shelters the privileged must have, his belief that there is a chosen group of egg-heads and their call-girls with entry permits to subterranean shelters who will people and revive the smashed globe after the holocaust. In this wilderness the conversation sounds insane, but it is not so insane and the insanity of it is dismissed when Colley remarks on a bomber exercise that took place a week before I came home. "So low," he is saying, "I nearly ran off the road. In my own country, I am nearly run off the road by low-flying operatives from the States. I've made a map of this country and marked on it all the places from which Australians are barred by foreign military authorities. North West Cape. Pine Gap. Honeysuckle Creek."

"He was beaten up," Emmeline interjects, her long hair dripping forward over her muted features, "outside two of them by some big American security guards."

"That's right. Broke my camera. Threatened legal action."

We coddle our rage. Or they do. I am more interested in the specifics of Colley and Emmeline and Timothy Rider.

Her father talks about her, but only in a dad way and later, as I give Timothy a lift back to town, his bike slung in the back of the van, he talks about the father.

He talks and I see Emmeline Colley in her spanking new uniform at the conservative boarding-school on the coast, given hell because of a scholarship and learning

42

fast not to be first with the right answers, the wittiest essay, hiding her cheap underwear and the brush and comb set from Woolworths, sitting alone under the mosquito damp of the figs in the lower playground, listening to the crack of tennis racquets. "Emmeline doesn't seem to fit in," they had written on her first school report, "and the early promise of her work does not seem to be realized."

"I contemplated withering," she had told Tim gravely as they lay stretched out by the lake's edge.

"She doesn't appear to be withering now," I say to Tim, and I feel him look hard at me.

Tell me about her Dad, Tim, about the smile, about her dead mum. How they came to be here?

Colley, Tim said, was another blow-in, a summer camper on the fringe of the lake and Wafer's wild theories. I paraphrase. In another time and with more aristocratic genes he might have been a successful flaneur, a con, a wide-lapelled spiv. But he was nothing much, so I deduce, except a failure at frankness. With a smile. He had given me the smile over coffee, as we said good-bye, that old smile her mother must have known and that Emmie knew like her alphabet, the charm of lop-sided incompetence that had brought him finally to this, a serf's pension in a no-hope landscape, the bummer's Eden.

He couldn't stick at anything, Tim said Em said. "Think it's time to move on, dear," he would say to the long-gone mum. "The job's getting to me." Meaning the charm that so engaged people when he met them – the alert grey eye, the quick practised smile, the quirked eyebrow – was failing to excuse a transparent indolence that worked like an itch on ambitious colleagues. He'd begun as a company architect in a Melbourne firm. There was some trouble with a trust account. "They simply don't appreciate an eye for investment," he'd said to his wife, to his drinking mates, to the cabbie who helped him move his office trash. "No vision. I think it's time to move on." He'd come to Sydney and a suburban practice on the north shore that never took off. The lonely buff walls of his waiting-room with copies of *Das Haus, America Now*, were awash with a beige light like water through which came the ever-present whine of the dental drill in the office next door. Tooth after tooth. Straightening a virgin blotter. Making phone calls to himself.

"I think it's time to move on," he put out as a tester to the girl who didn't do his typing for him, who didn't take the calls. "This doesn't seem to be working out." He'd given her the brightest and the saddest of his smiles that he preserved for really difficult occasions and had taken her to lunch on a borrowed twenty dollars. Severance lunch, he called it, and this time Emmie's mum said she really didn't know and would it be all right if she took a job herself and he said my dear and went red and said something would turn up and he wouldn't couldn't have his wife working for God's sake it lacked trust he simply had to know he had her trust or what else would . . . "Trust me," he said, giving her the smile and the practised quirk when she would have understood a blow better. "Do trust me. If you don't trust me."

From the distance of the outcast Colley would see his past and his future with a clarity of simply involved detail between the knitted smiles: the five room bungalow, the blue tea-caddy, the complete set of Dickens. And every other house held its caddy, its books. She had said, "Think of me. If you won't think of yourself. Think of me and Emmie. I'm the one who has to feed us all. The never-drying breast," she added bitterly. "Emmie can't understand what's happening."

There'd been a smell of horse and dung behind the stables in the country town where they'd first met. He was dogsbody in university holidays for her dad in a law practice that covered three fly-bitten townships. "Anything for you," he'd said. "Oh I'd do anything. Cross the Simpson Desert on my knees."

"Anything?" The word had escaped in echo from her like a sigh of total wonder while the horses snuffled in their boxes and the roar of the picnic race crowd made their privacy whole. "You know, I can't really believe that. Not really."

"Why?"

"No one ever."

"Ever what?"

"Ever does anything so — so complete. They say it. They only say it."

"Watch me," he'd said, and wobbled away on his knees, on the gusts of her won laughter over the flattened ground behind the stables.

Think of me. Yes. Colley thought and then he hadn't thought, not beyond his smile, so many years had come between the horses snuffling and the blue caddy on the dresser. Move on to Malaysia and a construction camp near Kalianda where he came down in the world another little piece and was foreman of works on a building site for a tourist complex. The second floor collapse of the staff building wasn't really his fault, he was quick to explain. He had most certainly allowed for subsidence in the monsoon season. He threw a lot of technicalities at them about clay residues and absorption ratios. But the rains. Screw died on the third day and none of the men wanted to speak to him after that though he kept trying to chat them up in the company bar, and the years narrowed to a sullen walkway between their narrowed look-away eyes. Who did that? the master had roared across the assembly lines wilting in the playground heat. I want you to know, the master roared, that I regard you as all to blame, everyone of you, for this conspiracy of silence. "Conspiracy of silence," the master had repeated, rolling the cliché around his tongue as if it were a lolly. "Unless one of you comes forward . . ." And Colley had been that one, and after that, there had been the isolation his smile couldn't crack, the extended foot, the sudden onsets in quiet corners of the yard.

Thirty years on, the fecund decay of the tropics became his own scent.

"I think, Colley, it's time you moved on," the manager said, fussing with some papers on his desk in the makeshift office. And the secretary was in ear-shot too. "There's nothing for you here now. The firm appreciates you made a genuine error but there isn't room for error."

No room for error and the chaps at the club all moving aside. Christ, he could empty a room these days three minutes flat and the bar-girl soggy and beautiful with oriental tears because Screw had told her a lot of lies and laid her.

Even his typist, that other typist that other time, had picked indifferently at the oysters sitting there at Watson's Bay with the sun bouncing round on an endlessly sanguine harbour, striking over the smell of sand and salt. Screw had been tangled up with one of the girders and the ambulance bogged down on the road to Palembang.

"What will you do?" he had asked his typist at the severance lunch, watching her careful carmine nails pull crabbily at a lobster claw.

"Don't worry about me," she had said. "It's you. You're the one to worry." A prophet in her own typing pool, he thought sourly, as he waited his week out in Palembang, waiting for clearance papers and a plane, the air green with rain and the river coming up and the stink of ripe and rotting fruit.

Back to the mainland and one casual job after another,

46

not pretending to be an architect any more: salesman, shop-assistant, door-to-door — the smile and almost the foot cut off by its closing, Emmie up to his shoulder now and his wife nursing her hopelessness and a secret cancer that was to tick on for three more years.

They moved from brick to timber to fibro, chasing down the social building ladder till they ended up renting an inner city apartment just off lower William Street before it became trendy: two rooms and a bath stuck above the prostitutes and the sex shops and the pushers and his wife nursed her hopelessness and gradually gave up wanting the houses she had pored over in *Home Beautiful*, the grove of fruit trees, the lilac mist across some timber pergola.

Colley slid down the job-ladder as easily as a man on a greased pole, keeping his lop-sided smile and alert blue eye whacking around unattainable horizons in the sweating Sydney summers, till he reached casual labouring jobs on the road.

"It's not right," his wife had protested one exhausted evening of a dusty December as Emmie hung out the living-room window of the flat watching curiously the trade in flesh that passed below. And Colley, who now loved his daughter more than he loved his wife, hoping, clinging to the idea that she had not yet discovered his uselessness, shuddered at her tensed and inquisitive small-girl shoulders and agreed.

Move on to a bauxite town on the Gulf and only two weeks of purple cloud run the locals called Morning Glory before he had the accident that shattered his right leg just below the knee.

Patched up, he had a limp that matched the eye, the smile, the charm.

"He's all of a piece now," his wife said to Emmie. "All of a piece."

The day he half-fell, half-stepped into their van after

47

the Coast hospital finally discharged him, he said, "Well, old girl, you've certainly cracked the jackpot in me. My dear," he said, and let her have a tear above the smile as he took her hand and squeezed it. "It could have been all so different."

"No," she said. "No. It couldn't ever have been different with you."

The remark made him momentarily bite his lip but the workers' compensation gave him enough to cure lip-biting and move on with style — a trim little camper-van fitted out with twee.

He packed his family aboard and took two months off to see the country.

"Holiday this time," he said. "Hey, Emmie?" And tickled her skinny ribs.

"Hasn't it always been?" his wife asked wearily. "I don't want to."

"Don't want to?" He couldn't believe her.

"No. I just want to stay put somewhere for a long time. I want to stay in one place. I want Emmie to make friends. I want to see something I've planted grow. I don't even mind if I don't get to know people. I've given that hope up. But I would like to know a landscape. Just one little piece of land down to its last leaf ant grub. All the bumps on the skyline whichever way I look. All of that. Is that too much?"

He didn't answer.

"Well, is it?"

"Over-familiarity," he joked badly. "It would breed most deep-seated contempt."

"They call it home," she said.

So they toured and toured and after three months, on the rim of desolation, she put her foot down.

"This is it," she stated, her mouth in a new and dangerous ironic line.

There was a lake between two scrubby spurs, great

banks of dusty gidgee and a dying township, ten miles north.

"But I like it," he said, unaware of irony. "I do like it."

They leased a block running down to the lake and though the ironstone grappled with soil, his wife started a garden, in rhythm with the secret enemy she knew to be within and which she ignored. Colley began to build a house and though his theory was better than his practice, and despite a game leg, he achieved three rooms and a kitchen before he fell back exhausted.

It came to him one morning as he watched his thinning wife watering the dying plants with an absorption that would not recognize failure, that even should he want to leave, she would stay.

Emmeline was sent to boarding school on the coast and Colley sat over a set of books on fossicking that he had written away for, drooped quietly on his little verandah and made his wife endless cups of tea.

Gradually the lake-sheen moved across and blurred images of the rising river, the rain, the stench of weeds, though every now and then, at nights especially, he was over by the chart-room hearing the first warning creak of girders and seeing nothing but the ugly angles of collapsed iron, concrete and mud and the rain never stopping while the boys in the bar kept their secret huddles and not even the pleading blaze of his smile could scorch them into speech, his secretary fastidiously picking at a lobster claw and the old copies of *Das Haus* blowing in a wind off the Harbour, page after page riffling open at the soft-core porn of houses of the month.

It's all an impossible clamber to exist in the mind of anyone else, I decide, as I pick this bit and that from Tim, from Jam, from Emmeline herself. But Colley is beginning to exist in my mind along with his waif-like daughter, with Timothy Rider, with Wafer, with Moon.

As I discover my mind to be peopled, I realize I am no longer bored.

49

Perhaps I am in love, this week before Christmas.

My small world suddenly has vigour.

I am painting Emmeline Colley surrounded by tidal waves of school girls.

I am painting Father Colley, quirkily grinning at crashing walls, a misty dead wife, a secretary who handles lobster claws with ennui. I paint him drinking alone. I paint him smiling at his daughter. I am finding the timbre of this township and enjoy, unexpectedly, swapped good mornings, exchanges at the store, dignified weather platitudes with Councillor Brim, Headmaster Rider, Sergeant Cropper. I shock the lot of them by dropping in on Rosie Wonga with a pile of childhood picture books for her boy.

This is really being in love. My day sings.

Paint is hardly the word. Line drawings. I cannot yet bear to assemble colour in case it betrays me. It is the state of my mental health.

Monochrome. Interesting blurscapes of sepia and grey.

It's time to tell you about Doss. This whole horrible canvas will have the detail of a Brueghel and the alarm of Goya.

If I tell you that Doss is a big-breasted blonde of coarse good nature, you'll say I am stirring a worn-out image.

Nevertheless. Behind her was a string of lovers and husbands littering the years all the way back to the libertarian groupies of the forties. After the left-wing push at the Cross she'd moved out and away. "I've done the island bit, lovey," she would say, had said, once I'd reached my unshockable girls-together teens. "The fossicking bit, the posh little boutique, the gallery crappery. The lot. Now I'm here. And I don't bloody mind it. Too old to move on, lovey. Too bloody old."

An early lover had seen her through a year of coral atoll vistarama.

"It was terrible," she said. "Terrible. After the first two months. Scratching for sand crabs, running out of water, sand-flies, the out-board cracking up and three cans of beans on the bush-shelf larder. Islands might sound marvellous, lovey, but that's another myth. Like men. They're the biggest myth of the lot. God! When I look at all those screaming Arab males on telly, I wonder what it would be like if men were the emotional sex." And she'd shake with laughter.

"Well, after that, dear? Let me see. Oh. I met a prettier man, I suppose, with a prettier car." And she'd give a sly look.

Marriage took her opal fossicking round Coober Pedy and after privations had speeded up the palling process she drifted away from the big-muscled miner who no longer excited her and back in Sydney ambled easy, easy, through a series of fly-by-night businesses while she raked some capital together. "Not again, love," she would protest when this one or that suggested marriage, half an eye on her purse. "I've had the marriage bit, too. And it's getting too late for kids. Me with the Milo! I ask you."

"You're not womanly, Doss," one outraged man had cried. ("Thought I was rich, dear. And I have to admit that I did have a bit. Yes. Quite a bit!") "Not an ounce of the woman in you."

"There's plenty of ounces," she told me she had said to him. "And they're all sexy." I could sense his outrage twenty years on. "Oh yes, I said to him, 'Listen, buster, it's always been the same for your lot to have it your way. No sweat. No pack-drill. Not a tuppenny cuss for the woman you sleep with, the kids you sire. If there's anywhere in the world one of you who actually likes women or kids, the rest of you think he's unnatural, a poof. It's manly not to care. My God, how manly! So I play it your way and I'm the unnatural one. According to you. But believe me, oh do believe me, I'm not playing. I just am that way. Am. And you don't like it. Well, we've had to put up with centuries of it played your way and now you can't tolerate one little outbreak of honesty from the other side. The enemy. Buddy, you'll just have to tolerate it. Shove off!' "

Ten years after that, believing she had exhausted all the categories of bliss, Doss settled, more from exhaustion than desire, for a hit and miss relationship with a man who was flung quite literally through her windscreen. She had been puttering absent-mindedly along a north coast backroad in a dewy midnight that fogged the windscreen when a motor-bike rose from nowhere over the hill, swerving like a dancer; and though she braked into a languorous skid it was too late to avoid the impact and glass storm that broke all about her as the rider thudded head-first onto the bucket seat at her side.

"Saved by grog," she commented, "always saved by grog. And ruined by it. He never knew what hit him."

An errant sense of responsibility took over her judgement after she had made a couple of duty hospital visits ("Like a lush background of cellos," she told me. "Fuddled my mind.") to check his scarred progress, and later, after she had teamed up with Stobo, she would always turn the explanation of their partnership into a joke, an apologetic joke, perhaps even a sad one, but a joke.

Oh the tears of things.

Where are you now, Doss, with your brassy front, off-colour jokes, ribbing the reps who came by, corseted to bust, the blonde hair set in jazz age waves, your eyes blue and hard, but twinkly? Where's Freddie Stobo, pint in hand, leaning boozily across the bar to inspect a stranger passing through?

If I could only move the town and the folk in it back to square one — four weeks, five, a year — before Christmas.

Why do I keep calling it a town? Is it because of what it once was? Its ghost is barely a settlement of a handful of stickers and stayers. While you put together my sketches of them, I simply go on painting.

I am painting Emmeline Colley in the flesh.

There is a *largo* droop to the shoulders. Hair repeats the motif. The eyelids shadow blue.

Smiler is in his kitchen fixing coffee. At break-time my patient sitter talks about herself while her dad makes outside noises at a dying vegetable patch, still smiling. Emmie, surprisingly, produces a private note-book for adult opinion.

Why me?

I read:

> The birds come like heart-beats to perch on trees growing from my head. Small brown birds when they should be red. In the next house the man shakes a table-cloth that shyly they fly into and they're caught, rolled up in blue.
>
> Later, he will make a singing candelabra of them, each one lit with the flame of its high cry.

I read it. I do not know what to say. I daren't say,

"What does it mean?" and as if Emmie had guessed these might be my lying words, she says slowly, "Later on, when you think about it, you'll know what I was trying to say."

But I know now.

I turn to the next page, unwillingly, slowly, as if I am turning an inevitable moment of Wafer's history, or hers, or mine.

Emmie's breath is light as she leans near my shoulder, smelling of high summer.

I read again:

I hold the lake up to my face
I see nothing
I switch it to catch the light
I see ships I shall never board
Towns I will never visit
People who will never know my name.

O brilliant Emmeline Colley! How could I cope with a girl like you?

Tell us about your Dad, Em, about the smile, about your mum, how you come to be here?

I am merely checking.

Mr Wafer appears on the dying syllables of Smiler's welcome and stands watching Emmeline and me sipping our coffee, playing ladies, and moves over to the canvas and remains dreadfully still. "You do her justice," he compliments me at last. And behind him comes Timothy Rider crashing his bicycle to bed on the verandah steps.

Timothy watching Emmeline, watching Wafer watching Emmeline, watching the protrait with its hazy blues, a stilled light within its centre.

"It reminds me," Timothy says judicially, his handsome face pulled down in thought, "of Wafer's stone."

I am not sprung! I'm flabbergasted that unconsciously I've derived simile from the secretive lump of gem Wafer has in his house. Given to omens, I suspect. My mind tumbles the rock about and polishes its corners until the bold purple of it, the centre fire of blue catches me by the shy corner of an eye.

"No. That wasn't intended." I'll say nothing more. I give Wafer a wisp of a smile and all he says is, "It's a pretty thing."

"'The gemstone?" Smiler asks coming in from the summer.

"Both."

"Both?"

Timothy Rider steers Emmeline's daddy towards my canvas.

"See. The painting. The stone."

"And the sitter," I say, my generosity hurting. "Three pretty things."

What is the matter with me? Wafer, I have sketched you out of my system — or is it into? A bomb nut with a stunning indifference not only to my style but to almost everyone's. It's that indifference that makes me rage. All my life I've only had to squeak for notice and now, when I would cry out louder than at any other time, his slow and measured comments on our spinning globe make me feel the foolishness of frenzy. Even the frenzy of paint.

I am in love with the town.

I want it to be bird-shot with good mornings as I walk its one street.

I am happy that the grey-blue of scrub-box is its own snow.

I say Good morning, Father. Good morning, Jam. Good morning, Tottie. Good morning, Sergeant Cropper, Councillor Brim, Headmaster Rider. I say Good morning, Doss, Freddie. I am Madame Bountiful with boxes of lollies for Rosie and her tribe of dead-beats, with beautifully wrapped books for Timothy and Emmie and a dinner invitation for Mr Wafer.

Father sprawls in his squatter's chair after dinner grasping a Scotch like a hand grenade. Jam is pretending to plait a new stock-whip. We look listlessly at national television until there is a documentary on America's MX installations and I feel Wafer quiver like a dog. There are war-games in Europe, says the nine o'clock newscaster, a meat racket has been uncovered, ("Now what will you do with all those Roos, dad?" Jam jokes) and there is to be a special programme on how to avoid the worst effects of radiation. And even later, I suggest, there'll be a fashion-flash on après-bomb wear.

Father is excited with all the paraphernalia of aggression. He becomes charged with adrenalin.

"And what shows were you in?" he asks Wafer.

"None," Wafer says modestly.

"None?" shocked father asks. "How did you manage that? Vietnam? Korea? None of those shows?"

"I've spent my life draft-dodging," Wafer says. I can only admire his nervous honesty. Father grips his Scotch tightly and takes a heavy pull at it.

Then he begins to laugh, having to turn such an outrage into a joke. "My God," he says. "My God. Bit of a humorist, eh?"

The television screen is exploding with smoke, supersonic missiles and sinking nuclear submarines. The picture cuts to a hawkish suburban matron who threatens to take a gun to anyone invading her shelter. "I have the children to think of," she says. She is wearing a salon permanent, a John Valentine body and a Pucci slack-suit.

Wafer has become very pale.

"This appals me." He indicates the rocking screen.

"One of those Commie pacifists, are you?" father asks rudely. He is not a "good" drinker. Any moment now he will quote George Custer and say "The Army is the Indian's best friend". "There is no way," he goes on, licking his lips at a particularly spectacular mushroom cloudburst, "that we can underestimate our defence strengths. No one likes these things. No one wants them." He was giving his version of the reasonable man. "But we simply have to have them."

"But these sorts of things?" Wafer asks, looking at a volcano of flame. "These? There won't be anyone who has to have them after the generals have flung a couple of warners around."

"The army," father says, paraphrasing, "is the child's best friend."

Well, that was unfortunate. Wafer remembers bits of his daddy littering a small street off Bishopsgate.

A kind of blaze crosses his face and subsides.

"I couldn't even begin to tell you what a child needs. Not begin. If I begin we'll argue and it's — it's too close to Christmas."

He sat back in his armchair as if he had wrestled with a mine-blow of vehemence and won but I am ashamed of his intellec ual timorousness? cowardice? before my family.

The television screen is ablaze as well.

"There'll be one thing you won't need," father says kindly, nodding at the turmoil in the box. "A shelter. It will be all in, all in. Complete erasure for the lot of us. This little globe will have to start again from scratch."

"You don't think —" Wafer seemed angry — "that the hit men, the political mafia who run the world, east *and* west, and working together behind the scenes, don't have their underground food barns, stock stables, reservoirs and technical machines for the aftermath, do you? The big emergence. It will be like passing the animals out of the Ark onto Nebo, only there'll be feudal overlords with survival packs who'll get the whole thing going again and the poor wretches of survivors, if there are any, with their sickness and their sores, will be willing slaves for a can of uncontaminated beans. Oh I can see the lot."

Father is shocked into silence and Jam says, putting the whip aside, "Then there's only one solution. Only one."

"What's that?"

"Head for the centre of the blast. It's what I'd do. Quicker. Instant ash."

"My dad did that," Wafer says. "Unwittingly."

Of course that remark should have caused embarrassment, confusion, but a red-tab man is ready for anything and the evening was whittled away with a paternal monologue on balance of power, the rules of international warfare (I had to laugh), the emerging black nations and the threat they posed to clean-skins like us.

All to the accompaniment of Wafer's paling smile.

Something had to shock the moribund evening alive.

"Wafer has a shelter," I say.

Jam rolled around with laughter.

Five days before Christmas a circus train passed through, a road train of six large trucks for the animals and a clutch of caravans and trailers. They shook their way along our little piece of scarred blacktop and took the road to Mainchance.

Two miles out, the van carrying the lions and one sad tiger dropped a wheel over a narrow culvert into a creek-bed and overturned. The recent rains had made the banksides into brown glass. Allbut, enchanted with the vision of man-eaters head over arse, drove out en masse with sandwich packs and brownies to sustain while we stared or helped.

Nothing helped. The skid-runs on the creek bank deepened and when late afternoon settled into twilight, the cage was still end up. The town's one tractor had broken down hours before and there we were with twenty stranded circus folk, an elephant that had begun to trumpet, half a dozen horses and five yowling big cats.

Councillor Brim's large-pored nose was swollen with the fuss of it.

"I don't know," he said. "I simply don't know. We've rung Mainchance and they can't get a crane out until tomorrow. We can't possibly cope with you all, food, beds, and so on, you know how it is. And we simply can't have you camping here on the trunk road. The only

60

thing you can do is to take the rest of the circus on and leave someone here to keep an eye on the cats."

The circus owner was a stringy man with worried rims to his eyes and a mouth that, when closed, was merely a fretful line drawn above his chin.

"Why?" he demanded. "What the hell's wrong with us staying here?"

"What's wrong?" Councillor Brim echoed irritably. "It's not on. Not on at all. All the land round here for the next forty miles is private grazing land. It's a question of permission. A question of permission."

"Well, get it then," the man said.

"And I don't think," Brim continued, ignoring him and coming to the nub of the matter, "it would be advisable considering the problem we have already with the blacks. We have a big black problem, you know. Your men. The women. There could be trouble."

His mouth pinched prettily.

"Isn't there a town common, or something?" the man persisted. "A bit of crown land tucked away somewhere? Where's all this bloody country friendliness we hear so much about? Where's that, eh?"

"You'll have to move on," Sergeant Cropper intervened. He swaggered up to the little man in the fading light, flexing his authority. "Like right now."

"Fair go," the man said. "You can't expect us to do that tonight. There's another sixty miles over a hell of a road."

"We've told you what you can do," Sergeant Cropper said. It was time he took over. "Okay, now. Let's get these things moving."

"Stuff you," the circus owner said.

To Cropper's and Brim's departing backs.

Then the town group, our group, began to drift their guilt away, fading strategically into evening, with tiny stinks of dust and petrol and the rain starting; and as I drove back in the family truck arguing with Jam — after all, it was our land they had bogged down in — Wafer drove by and Wafer stopped and it was Wafer who made them welcome and convoyed their road-train out to the lake and let them camp the night.

Perhaps that was really the first moment of war, that deliberate flouting of Sergeant Cropper. Perhaps he wanted a war. A man in search of the perfect bomb shelter must have reason for search, must have an excuse for his excuse. Radio daily brought us the constants of twentieth century living — neutron bombs, ICBMs, MX missile shelters — but it was going to be this survival from the middle ages, this shabby back country circus that lit our town's fuse.

For next morning there was a rape.

Councillor Brim on his way to the council chambers, making an early start to clear up a non-existent backlog of paperwork before Christmas, happened to glance proprietorially into the window of the tiny haberdashery run by his wife and discovered to his disgust that the two dummies in their modest summer prints had been sexually molested. The evidence spread in horrible stains down the fronts of their out-dated dresses and in small drying messes on the floor. The front door of the little shop swung listlessly as if sated in the early breeze that blew down the main street, inspecting paper scraps, stirring the grass beside the monument.

"Oh my God!" Brim said, clutching the door frame as he took it all in. "Oh the animals."

Sergeant Cropper was inclined to laugh. He heard out the other man's complaints, inspected the spoorless premises and said, "Well, write it down to experience, mate," and laughed again, openly. "They were bloody awful frocks," he said. "Saks of Boong Avenue."

"It's those circus louts," Brim kept repeating. "They must have come back."

"You want me to check?" Cropper inquired. "You want me to check on the fellow with the lions?"

He drove off in mirth, drove easily out along the road towards the culvert but braked hard when he saw the circus train coming out from the dam turn-off. Furious, not with the mischief done Mrs Brim's shopware but a defiance of his orders that seemed a greater indecency, he waited until the last van had trundled off on the road to Mainchance, then whipped his rage down the dam track to Wafer.

Tearing strips off Wafer, so I hear later that morning, above or under the Wagnerian pulse from the stereo, the whump from the generator.

Immune to Hunding's theme, Cropper stood his bully-boy ground and I see him towering huge above the funk-hole of all time, his yob crescendo vilifying the world.

"But ultimately it's you they blame," I told Wafer.

He too was inclined to smile. Weren't we all?

"No matter," he said. No matter? In a town like this?

I can vision cops and councillors striding the upland country of the Australian nightmare, lurching over dream canvases of drought-rind with the whole throbbing blue of the zenith trapped behind bars.

Wafer continues to inspect the morning while I work in my sketch-pad. I am drawing Wafer and this sketch, done from the flesh, not my memories of it, will be the only record I am ever to have. The early day seems to have no planes to it, no design, is formless and hot; and then across its mirage-flickering sunniness a small stick figure, arms legs hair at disjuncted angles, comes running jerkily across the far lake rim towards Wafer's ungrown orchard, between the aisles of small trees, driving herself and her panic, we can see now, upwards to the house.

Quickly I add the stick-figure to my sketch and then Wafer is gone from me before I can breathe my surprise and somewhere below me on the path catches the naked Emmie in his arms.

She'd gone down to the water-hole that morning, she gasps, and even as she gasps out her story I remember rapture, my own holiday discovery fifteen years before of a place where she-oaks dangled their hair over a perfect circle of creek-fed water before the little creek moved out of its stone tank and itched its way to the dam.

I am too far from it, from those swimming-pool mornings, the water secret and green and my own body white as peeled grass skimming from one bank to the other in less than six strokes. And there was a boy.

Not even his name remains.

But of the three or four images that have had the power to stir my bored blood across the years, that pool is one. Not the lake with its overt mirror of upside-down sky, but that small green tank and a clumsy brushing of mouths that forces me to cry back through terrible distances and fifteen years. Wafer, I cry now through other distances. What happened? What made me do what I did? The awkward words put out too late on paper, lurching their spastic feelers across pages you can never see, admissions you can never answer. Emmie! My one-time letter to you and you never answered. Why should you? And the visit, that time, to your school, the headmistress curious in the vestibule behind the wary screen of her glasses.

"She is no longer with us."

"No longer with? You mean she has left?"

"That is exactly what I mean. Was the matter urgent? You are a friend, I take it, of the family. Well, little enough family, really. The poor child's mother died some time ago. Is it really urgent?"

Oh for me, for me it was urgent, the nagging spur of confessional lust.

"Are you feeling unwell?" she had inquired leaning forward in her headmistress chair to me bent painfully in mine.

"No. Only a spasm. A moment." Trying Colley's smile, the old dad's, the old Smiler's — here's to you, Emmie's dad!

"Emmeline left last term."

"Do you know where she has gone?"

Too blunt.

"Please."

She regards me with reproving but inquisitive eyes. Her grey hair is waved neatly behind her ears.

"Do you mean what school? What place?"

I make apologizing noises. She is not really placated.

"I'm sorry. I can't really help you at all. Her father called for her a week or so after term commenced. And he gave no reasons. I don't know," she added, slowly removing her glasses so that her myopia protected her, "why I'm telling you this. Is there anything the matter?"

How could I explain Wafer, Moon, my treachery? There is everything the matter, I wanted to tell her, wanted to sob, despite the carefully understated little suit, despite a long-lost prefect's badge and the faded pocket colours of an athletic wunderkind. I need absolution and forgiveness and I cannot speak about it at all to anyone but Emmie who could pronounce the *absolvo te*, if she would, and take me back, if only into the fringes of the groves of ordinariness again.

(Oh where are the te deums of my youth, the high voice at the peak of ecstasy?)

So she gasps out her story.

She had been at the pool less than an hour before.

I see her plunge into the heart of the tank, rising, shaking her water-straightened hair, floating with occasional fin-flick, all as I used to do, staring into green with eyes half-closed under the rhythm of the little waterfall, a half-smile about her mouth, not her father's smile, I concede, never that bright lying smile that made me as well as Emmie want to weep for him.

(I wrap Emmie's distress in a towel.)

Emmie keeps gabbling out horrors.

It was the smallest sound of pebble-splash close to her left arm that disturbed her, flung like a deliberate word.

She swung over in a second, her toes just finding the sandy bottom, aware that the stillness outside the gobbling of the waterfall was too still. About the edges of the pool nothing moved except the small partings and closings of the strands of she-oak, yet she could sense paused movement all around. Standing in the water, shivering a little and waiting, poised, she heard at last what she knew she had been waiting for: the crunch of boot on the pebble slope just behind the trees.

The step was measured, deliberate, and, as she watched, Moon's head and shoulders grew odiously between parted branches, then his whole body loomed to straddle her heap of clothes on the bankside.

She gasped her fear at us. Instantly I am painting Emmie anew.

Moon's face was wiped clean like a dreamer's, his lost eyes fastened on her in wordless one-intentioned gravity and she knew then that he had been standing back there in the screen of she-oaks watching for some time. As she tells us I am conscious of her changing body, of periods, of half-formed breasts.

She lowered herself imperceptibly into the water so that it lapped now about her shoulders, bracing her feet against the shifting sand for flight but sensing that might be an error. It was the nothing on his face, she kept saying. The nothing.

"I didn't hear you," she had accused. "I didn't hear you come."

Something instructed her to make it sound natural: talking to Moon of the vegetable patch, the Moon who had helped Smiler with fencing, the Moon who tinkered around with the generator.

He didn't answer. His feet ground down the last ten feet of the slope impressing the total of himself upon her, the shoulders, the flanks lean in stained work-shorts, the snake boots laced up tightly around his ankles.

"Get out," he had ordered. "I want to talk to you."

The pool shudders for me. Already his hands were moving at the waist-band of his shorts, his eyes never leaving the pale oval of her face as it floated above the surface of the pool.

"I don't want to have to pull you out," he said vaguely.

His own wore an improbably distant look and she could not know that this glade and those other glades were becoming one blurred image of past impulse and invention.

He kicked his shorts to one side, threw his work singlet on top of them and even as she floundered back he was in the water and gripping her arms, forcing her upright against his tautened muscle. Chin to chin and his beard was hideously soft around a smell of peanut butter she would later recall as sad.

She could not speak. Her mouth choked up with water. But her struggles spoke and he only waggled negatives, tightening his grasp of her, drawing in a huge breath, holding it as he pulled, as she tugged, while he examined her swivelling face.

The sigh he had taken in rushed out of him in a kind of sob.

He was mumbling something, *verte desnuda, verte desnuda*.

Those words, over and over and over, the grip tightening, his body forcing itself on her, then the both of them slipping, falling back through her fourteen years, him dragging her up again, forcing her up and back, back to the bank, his body acting as a ram, water streaming behind and the rattle of water-hen taking off across the lake behind the trees.

He shoved her half-way up the bank on skidding grass and pebbles, pressing her down under the light from his freckled eyes, the strange scar that raked from outer eyelid to ear, talking to her. She thought she heard herself crying then yelling, slimy with mud and water and the scalding points of his elbows stabbing brutally into her shoulders, his fingers threaded through her hair.

At that point Emmeline, I say formally, had managed to jab upwards with her knee, heard him grunt, felt his elbows lose pressure and raking out at his face with her nails clawed again and again at the blind eyes.

To see her naked.

As he jerked away she sprang past him, stumbling, reeling down the track that led over the spur and up to the house, screeching as she ran, not for the ineffectual smile, the dad-arms that ached with failure, but for Wafer.

"The rest of it means more," Wafer said, looking past Emmie at me.

"The rest of what?"

"That poem, those words," he was saying. *"Verte desnuda.* To see you naked is to remember the earth."

There is a natural synchronism in the world. All things crash together.

After Wafer and I had taken a calmed-down Emmie to her house we discovered that Smiler had dropped backwards from a step-ladder and injured his hip.

He lay on the floor where he had fallen with a smile of placating apology, eyes candid with admission of fault, of folly even. "God, Emmie," he said as we eased him from floor to stretcher and pondered the next move, "I am sorry to be such a bore."

Wafer ran him sixty miles to the hospital at Main-chance where the injury proved to be merely a disloca-tion of the steel pin from his former accident. A brave blue-eyed rueful grin, dismissing it.

"Emmie?" he remembers, catching his girl's eye as she stands at the end of his hospital bed. "What about Emmie?"

"I'll take her," Wafer and I say together. Emmie droops behind hair.

"That's settled, then," Smiler says, unaware, unaware.

Stobo is singing in a cracked baritone when Wafer drives

us back into Allbut. The voice pounds out hoarsely from the bar of the Wowser:

> Don't want no city
> Don't want no town
> Don't want no bright lights
> Folks get me down

Outside the pub, Wafer heels the van in gently to the verandah. Emmie is sleeping on a couple of blankets in the back and, as we sit there listening, Stobo's words become italics for a township that has staggered to the end of the line with its warped houses, its dead cars rusting quietly, the junk beneath the scrub-line along the road strip. My heart, surprisingly, cannot bear to part with such riches.

> My daddy's been bent
> My mummy's gone pro
> I long for a cool girl
> Without get up and go

Stobo sings with infinite good humour as we shove through the swing doors into the linoleum dusk of the bar. They've done something for Christmas, a scarlet ho-ho Santa and spray-on snow, strings of balding tinsel from light-fitting to walls. I feel the possibility of carols from Doss's radio but Stobo's song is more suitable for this lost town.

He breaks off, winks, says "How'd you be?" and snaps open a stumpy. He is an uninventive and prosaic barman and not even Doss's passionate lost years of the flatulent good life have done anything to increase the six bottle muster on the shelf behind him. She keeps them there now as a memento of the pub as she bought it: one bottle of each — gin, whisky, sweet sherry, port, rum and brandy. It's a matter of honour in the town that no one asks to be served from them and they remain holy objects, ikons of carnival.

There's only beer and more beer, the national nectar.

We sit in what used to be the ladies' lounge and through the open door to the front bar I can see a bunch of cattlehands who have driven in for a Friday night rort sitting up at the far end of the curved counter clapping and cat-calling Rosie Wonga's Ted who is dancing, stone-drunk tribal, waving and weaving with his famine-land limbs out of control, mashing the air with dark surrender flags. One eye is bunged up with sandy-blight, the other rolling chocolate and red jitters within its socket like a pin-ball. He's making singing sounds too, echoing Stobo, gulps, retchings and high laughter that switches to flash-rage when one of the stockmen thrusts out a leg and brings his corroboree flat on its face.

Ted Wonga crawls on all fours below the laughter. Doss holds one questioning glass. Blood and mucous stream from Ted Wonga's nose and there's a sudden hawking rush of vomit all over the stockman's boots.

"Shit!" the stockman screams. "Chuck the dirty bastard out."

He stands up and his fouled books kick nostalgically to the source.

"Filthy boong. Douse him."

Stobo rolls round the end of the bar.

"Well," he says, "you are a right lot of jokers." Ponderous, he surveys the mess. Ted Wonga is writhing in his slime. "Thanks for the clean-up job. Thanks a lot."

Wafer is leaning away from all this as if on the tearing edges of a high wind, forgetting the beer he is holding and doesn't want anyway, his mouth opening on impossible words.

"Come on, now," Stobo orders, glaring at the

cowhands, "that funny bugger who did this, give us a hand."

The men's faces flatten and harden. "Go stuff yourself," dirty boots suggest, recovering from the outrage of it. "Go get stuffed."

Doss leans her breasts across the bar and her shiny blue eyes snap.

"It'd be a damn sight pleasanter than if you did it," she says.

Stobo sighs, bending over the muck and grabbing the black under the armpits. He lugs him, trailing reek, towards the swing doors, shoulders them apart and hauls the puking Ted onto the verandah where he props him against the rail. He fills a bucket at the outside tank and comes back again to swill down the floor, splashing the circle of legs, boots.

"You lot," he says. "You funny lot," but they ignore him and in minutes, as if there's been no break, he's singing again:

So I'm leaving the city
This town's got me low.

Emmeline has sauntered out of sleep and into the bar, her eyes searching for us. Emmeline Colley, mother-naked in Wafer's paternal arms, writer of words that touch unknowns. A fly-specked Christmas is four days away round the corner, there is the seasonal madness working up to mince pies and I feel in my marrow that traditionalists like Mrs Councillor Brim are praying for a temperature of thirty-eight Celsius in their kitchens so that they can decipher the holy day with penitential joy.

A forlorn three-day bearded man is asleep at the next table, chair-slumped, legs out-thrust. He has slept through the previous scene, mouth gaping. He sleeps while Emmie comes in and while I let Emmie check-

72

mate me as she pulls a chair between mine and Wafer's. Wafer smiles gravely at Emmie and my own smile rots on its branch.

She does not smile in return. There's my challenge. She does not smile and the man at the next table snores movingly and honkingly under his moustache, his sporty face flushed with all the gamey ambience of reps' smoking-rooms, the suitcase of neatly folded samples, the quick scuffle with the hotel maid. Behind a strangling tie of simple vulgarity his throat is congested and I know he stinks of sweat and despair.

His own terrible snorts wake him, and a blood-shot eye opens and shuts rapidly, focusing our interest. Finally the eye weasels itself into light and he mumbles something about having a little nap, straightens himself, shakes his head into sense, and physical changes swing like predictable tides across the ruined cheerful features — a stretch of the neck, a hand adjusting the choker of a tie, a quick mop with a grubby hanky, a twist and shrug of the shoulders as he re-settles into his salesman self. "Yes, well," — and he includes all of us in his optic net — "this is a god-awful town." Confidentially. "God-awful, if you don't mind my saying so. Not that you would mind, could you, I mean you've got to be travelling through like me, simply travellers, though Christ knows where you'd travel *to*. Mind you, I'm only here for a day or so on business." Was he seeing fleetingly those cut-price samples, the patented lines of cosmetics, the throw-out frocks from the season before last, the shirts that shrank first time they hit water? "Not that there's much doing here," — he was getting into swing — "but you have to do it for these little places. God, it's only fair. Keep them in touch. That's one of my little rules. Keep them in touch. People out here."

He thought of them for a bit and seemed to be wondering why his drinking hand was empty. He looked at its hollow curve. "They deserve something," he added sentimentally, thinking of the shirts, the awful print dresses Mrs Brim sold to the blacks, the cold creams.

His recovery was stunning, the emergence of a gorgeous insect from the unlovely pupa that had hung horribly in the chair.

He inspected Wafer as if truly noticing him for the first time.

"What's your line?"

"Mine?" Wafer said. "Oh I haven't a line. I'm out of all that."

"Farmer?"

"No. Not a farmer. Not your sort of farmer."

"Not my sort. What sort, then? Grazier? Business man?" He stared. "Business! You'd be battling, wouldn't you?" he said rudely. "You don't really look like a business man if you'll pardon me." He was alert now, examining Wafer's flapjack shirt, the clean but unpressed jeans, the head-band, the untroubled but distant eye.

"I'm retired."

"My God!" the man persisted. "You can't be living here. You mean you *came* here? Sought it out? Jesus, I need another drink. You serious? Here?"

Wafer went out to the bar and bought the man a beer. Emmie and I together watch the cowhands finding Wafer curious.

The drunken rep put his hand out for the glass and took his grog like medicine in three quick gulps.

"That's better." He wiped his mouth with the back of his hand. "Thanks mate. Now tell me —" and he leant forward across the table and gave Wafer the straight-eyed look that never failed. "Confidentially, what's a chap like you doing here?"

"Confidentially, I'm doing a number of things." Wafer smiled. I smiled. Emmie smiled. "I'm gardening. Grow-

74

ing a few vegetables, that is. I'm reading. I'm being. I'm doing nothing."

The traveller looked shocked.

"You'll do that all right, mate. Here! Let me tell you. I've been here before. I know. Once a year I come through these parts and it gets worse. A steady god-marvellous rural decline. Every year. Worse and worse and worse. But I haven't seen you around before, I'm sure of that, and I never forget a face. Quite an asset, that, but I never forget a face. Thought you must be new here."

"My problem," Wafer said, "is I can never remember the faces. Oh I can remember the names, hundreds, thousands of them. I just can't remember the faces that go with them."

Emmie giggled.

"You're putting me on," the man said aggrievedly. His lower lip looked as if it might sulk. "My God, I can't wait to take the car out in the morning. Wouldn't dream of doing it at night. Sixty miles of corduroy. They call it gravel but it's up to shit. This time of year there's pot-holes as big as dunnies, if you'll pardon the expression, and sand-drifts and boulders the council keeps there like mementos. But why am I telling you? You'd know." He waggled his empty glass invitingly but no one offered to re-fill it. "Yes. Like the very same goddam rocks. Would you believe the same goddam rocks? Why, I even mark-ed a couple that were half way across the track three years back and they're still there the next time I come through and kiss an axle goodbye. You see that monu-ment out there? Seen what's on it? Well, that was there five years ago and I guess it was there five years before that. I wouldn't know. Wouldn't want to know. You drinking, you two?"

"No more," Wafer said. "Not now. We have to get over part of that road on the way home. I haven't been here all that long," he added with a wry almost apologetic smile. "But it suits me."

"Suits you!" the rep snorted disbelievingly. "Suits! You must have known some lousy places."

Going home Wafer told me he remembered then, right on cue, a downtown dump in San Francisco near the bus station, the Pacific mists coming in like cotton waste, the grimy drizzle of the rain endlessly on junkies and shovers and tarts, the shine of filthy kerbs under the prettiness of it all, of the city, and a third floor walk-up to a single room with double locks, the light on all day in the corridors, the furnace heating breaking down in mid-December and the six inch gap of the safety chain. Lights on all day and the man with the terrible cough in the room opposite, the corridors the colour of blood and the Polish landlady rattling her moneybags weekly with notions of grandeur. "The Pakistani delegation is to come," she would keep saying. "Your room. I'll need your room." In fall, spring, high summer, winter-low, she said it. "I've got the Swedish commission. The Ghanaian president. The West German science congress." "It's time, man," the black from the room opposite would croak between coughing spasms as they met by the trash chute, "it's time for the bomb."

"Yes," Wafer said to the rep. "Worse than this."

The rep honked and flapped an I-don't-believe-you hand at him, and called out to Stobo for another beer.

Stobo was still singing, singing as he pulled the beers, as he dug Doss in the ribs going past, as he brought the tray across:

Don't want no bright lights
Jive me no jive
City blues lay me
More dead than alive

" 'Don't want no bright lights'," the rep repeated with ferocious irony and tried to wink us in, Emmie and me. "Well, I'll see you next time round, if there is a next time."

On the verandah of the Wowser the abo still lay there sleeping now in his own soil, lightly, happily. Across the road Mrs Brim was ostentatiously locking her little shop.

"The more I slow down," Wafer murmured, to Emmie more than to me, "the more I feel I move faster."

She'd understand that, subtle Emmie of the blunted profile, poet of my receding youth. "Daybreak and sundown are moving so close together," Wafer was saying, "they might be one. Soon I won't be able, not able at all, to fit myself in between."

What should we do about Moon?

"I think nothing," Wafer decides.

"But it's a police matter."

"He knows we know," Wafer says. "There's his curb."

I have taken Wafer a painting for Christmas, a jocular sketch of the war memorial with its tribute wreath of beer cans. Does he savour the painting's ghostly statements?

We sit on his verandah in the very echo of those statements waiting for Christmas.

Emmeline is absent, Doss Campion having driven her to Mainchance to visit Smiler, but her presence drifts through the room like an inquiring fragrance.

We watch Moon striding lean across the hill's hip, unabashed, and coming to visit. He turns into Wafer's track, is lost for a moment behind some bushes and reappears at the foot of the verandah. He wants to borrow a brush-cutter.

There's plenty of room at this inn, of course, and before I have adjusted to Moon's dangerous sweat, he is shifting edgily from verandah to room, picking up this and that, setting down, full of unease and ready to strike.

"Where did you get this then?"

He is examining Wafer's talisman, an untasted drink in

his other hand. This is the first time he has ever entered Wafer's house and he is there to establish innocence. His eyes follow the light in the stone as he moves it about, discovering or seeming to discover a fiery chatoyancy in the lumpy blue.

Wafer joins him inside, mild, distant, almost amused. "I don't remember."

"Try," Moon says.

"Should I?" Wafer takes the lump of stone from Moon's tanned fingers as if he cannot bear the fellow to touch.

"I think you should," Moon says. "I really think you should. It's not any old rock."

Wafer appeared to give the matter thought but the glance, the double glance he gave me, spelled only amusement.

"On my way here," he said. "When I was trekking around looking for a place to settle. I picked it up back of here, somewhere. A year ago. I can't remember where."

"How far back? You must have some idea?"

Old tiger Moon, lean in his stained bush-shorts, bent under visible stripes of sun, curved like a questioning muscle.

"What a fellow you are," Wafer said with distaste for more than the question in his voice, "what a fellow for specifics." He began to invent a little story. "I'd stopped for lunch, parked by this hill creek, oh northeast of here I suppose, to boil the billy and have a kip. And while I was poking around for fire-stones, I found this. I liked the colour. I kept it purely for luck."

Moon could have been stymied by this for he stared into Wafer's bland child eyes and I could see him wondering whether Wafer was a fool? Careful? Innocent? Moon's face detailed years of dealing with men who were careful, men who concealed expensive knowledge at the back of their eyes, behind mouths deliberately cool. Genuine innocence, like madness, would be harder for him to handle, for an innocent might jump any way at all.

"More than pretty," Moon said taking the rock back from Wafer and drowning in blue. I watch him drown, his lips opening slightly for air. "Oh you do know what it is, don't you? You do know?"

"I don't," Wafer said. "Do you?"

There was a foreignness about Moon's slanting eyes, his bones. He licked his lips and we might not have been there.

"It's corundum," he said. "Sapphire."

Wafer pulled a face. "Oh come. So large. Such a mass of it. More likely it's crystal, quartz crystal."

The tailings of a material world.

Moon cocked his head to one side like a bird of prey. "No." Consideringly. "No. The weight for a start. The translucency. I know something about this." He could not bear to put the stone down but weighed it, rocking it up and down in his cradling hand. "Too heavy. Far too heavy."

Why are we talking with this fellow, I ask myself, after his attempt on Emmie? Wafer could care more than I do, could want to see Moon trap himself. But he appears to be maddeningly indifferent saying coolly, "Well it could be sapphire. But that isn't important to me. For me it's a symbol." He planted the word like a stamp on the other man's forehead. "Finding it, finding it and this place came more or less together. I saw it as my luck."

"And you were coming in from the north?" Moon had a remarkable capacity to nag.

Wafer's eyes grew absent. "I said that." He moved back from Moon as an artist might to get him in his sights and I could sense Moon's irritability mark impatient time. "I'd been on the road two days and hadn't seen a thing but scrub. No trucks. Desolation everywhere, and that night, in the sunset, everything was rose."

"Rose?"

"Like a stain on the mind."

As he examined then dismissed this remark, Moon's mouth twitched. The beige of the plains west of here was an enduring softness, a sort of emotional stroke, coming upon it, like a soft explosion in the brain.

Moon handed back the gemstone and began rubbing his hands together, strong neat hands of a quick and carnal presence, his eyes blanked out with possibilities.

"I believe in luck," he said. "But mainly bad. I've had plenty of that."

"There are always cycles."

"Not for me. Not till now." The glade. The river. The hot back room at Las Pequeñas Muertes. And now that green tank of the little creek. "And dull bad luck at that." Was he refusing to acknowledge the clearing by the river, the boat nosing in to the dripping jungle bank that I had recorded on canvas, the bearer's hands flying off into bleeding space like red stars? "There have been unavoidable things," he added, brinking on confession, "things I regret. What I want —" and he fought around for the right words — "is a blaze. Something that makes my day riper."

It would have been too savage to ask "like schoolgirls" and I didn't ask and Wafer walked across the room to a wooden saint he had been carving with a pocket knife and rubbed over the saintly folds of black bean with his hand.

"That's the right word, anyway," Moon said. "Riper."

He reached out and took up the lump of stone from the table where Wafer had put it and pressed it suddenly against his forehead to set the purple lights racing into his mind like blood. "One of these days —" and his smile stiffened like cardboard — "you'll have to take me to that place." He swung round and looked ardently at Wafer.

"Show me where. I might find, well, something. Luck. A fortune." His smile remained fixed.

In his stained shorts standing there deep in a puddle of thought, a puddle of sapphire light, his work singlet clinging over gapes of bronze skin, the rock against his brow becoming a milky blue or lilac, with a small camp-fire head burning back in those purple ranges as he swung towards the verandah and the light.

"At that last camp you made, if you could find it." Moon almost threatened.

Wafer laughed out loud, hauling Moon to earth in the harness of his amusement, and I saw Moon pale with anger.

"You see," Wafer was beginning to say, about to give Moon the full gun on the pointlessness of avarice when he saw and Moon saw Timothy Rider shoving his two-wheeler across the bottom track to the house and in seconds Moon had thrust the rock back onto the book-shelf but deeper, into a cave between books, so that its colour was snuffed.

That afternoon he went off in his van and was gone until Christmas eve while we saw him in the mirrors of our eyes tracking the waste a hundred miles out, scratching for his Eldorado.

The next day Wafer took the rock in to Stobo.

"What is it?" he asked.

"Sapphire," Stobo replied without a breath before his answer.

"A pity," Wafer said predictably. "I was afraid it might be."

Stobo did raised eyebrows at him, comic with a wipe-rag.

"Pity? What you mean pity? Where did you find it, anyway?"

"God, I don't know," Wafer said. "I can't remember. I'm not a fossicker. I don't chart my travels. Somewhere about on my first trip this way. I wasn't looking, remember, so how would I know. It doesn't mean a thing to me as a stone." He hesitated and then repeated what he had said to Moon. "It's my luck."

"Pretty valuable luck, mate."

Wafer couldn't be bothered explaining that he was here, that he was. What other need could he have? Doss came over, her fine olive skin tight beneath the pirate 'scarf she wore, and taking the lump of stone from Stobo's hands appeared to be warming her fingers on it.

"This is trouble, lovey," she said to Wafer. "Trouble."

"For me?"

"Well, they'll all know, won't they? It'll be round this town in a day. They'll pester you stupid. They're still bitten, all of them, with fossick fever. It dies hard in a town like this. Always dreaming of the big strike."

Emmie sat in the back parlour with us, sipping a slow lemonade, her head so turned that she could look out the window past us, always looking out and past. The youth of her shone through all the shallow curves of flesh and hair and watching I felt bleak and began to count my remaining days.

"And Moon's already gone a-hunting, has he?" Doss pursued. "He'll hate to come back empty-handed, that one."

"He needs to catch something," Emmie said coldly who since Monday had become older than her years, than mine, and arrogant in Wafer's safety. Not just the shelter of him or about him; the idea of the shelter that made the very idea of Wafer a kind of fortress.

"Maybe," Stobo suggested eagerly, "we should all go

hunting." And he gave Wafer his silliest and most challenging smile.

"Oh Christ!" Doss cried. "See what I mean? Grow up, you silly bugger. It's all mirage stuff. It's opening time in ten minutes so get your mind on the real golden soak, will you?"

Stobo picked up the piece of rock again and gave it several encouraging pats as if urging it to breed. "Think of it. We could all be rich. Stinking rich."

"Balls!" Doss said. "Oh balls!" And she flung off to open the bar.

"I came into a town once," Wafer said to Stobo. Perhaps he meant it for me as well. Emmie certainly swung her hair to catch his words. "Oh in another country. I was walking. It doesn't matter where. And ahead of me, in the early morning streets of this village, there was a grotesque cripple staggering along with the help of a stick. A foot at a time. His legs were both bent out from the thigh almost at right angles to his body. And every step he took was a problem in balance. He'd lurch, reel, recover, lurch, reel, recover, all with the most appalling contortions. But he kept going forward to wherever he was going. And behind him, about twenty paces back, was this schoolboy imitating him. Lurch, reel, recover. Lurch, reel, recover. And behind *him* there was a little knot of his satchelled friends giggling themselves stupid, trying to smother their snorts and their laughs. And the kid who was doing the mimicking kept turning to wave and grin and urge their laughter into greater chokings and while he was turning to look at them, he crashed flat on his face in the mud. So I went up to him, the schoolboy that is, and I asked him in my poor French if I could help him. And he must have understood me, because he scrambled up, covered in mud, and went red. And he told me 'Va te faire foutre.' Go fuck yourself."

"And the old man?" Emmie asked.

"Oh he got where he was going."

"What's the connection?" Stobo asked, blinking rapidly.

"Can't you *see*?" Emmie was impatient and transfixed by the story.

"No I can't," Stobo said sulkily.

"It's this chasing," Wafer explained. "What does it matter if this is sapphire or not? Think of all the powerful and the wealthy gone before us, squashed out like bugs. Time. Time does it. Or us passing through time. Why, people go on as if they were running for ever."

"Not just the powerful and wealthy," I said. "What about the millions who had damn all."

The weight of those millions, along with Wafer's sad fable, oppressed me in this back drink lounge with its green linoleum and the browning photos of pit-heads and local prize horses. Those steaming slums in Bombay, Egyptian slave camps, desert goat-eaters, Aztec and Maya minions who all once blew their noses, had constipation, worried about the kids and wondered what was for dinner — or if there was dinner; who grew, bred, achieved a new spear or sling or ankle-chain or a piece of cloth to woo a girl with, who tilled share plots in Hungary, swept gutters in Billingsgate, dropped from scaffolding in Venice and died without having made the shallowest dint on the inexorable spin of the world.

"And mattered," I added. "And never got their names in the papers."

"Convinced?" Wafer looks at Stobo, shifts his luck into his shoulder bag.

"It won't do me. I've never had the glimmerings. Not of your sort of abstract luck. I can't understand it. I want something I can grip in my hand, like so. Can't understand, matey, how to use your sort."

"But you do understand," Emmie interrupted. She looked coldly at Stobo, resisting the mournful brown eye he turned doggily on her under the screech wave of

Doss's summons from the front bar. "What did you come here for if it wasn't to be a desert father?"

Wafer laughed with delight. "Do you think," he managed, still chuckles and nods at Emmie, "that the desert fathers were fossickers for more than the gold of God?"

Stobo looked hurt. "And you can cut out the father stuff," he said. "I've got a lease back of here. But there's nothing on my patch. Nothing. I've combed it through and through. Doss and me, we're stuck with this pub for a bit of security."

"You just want to pick a fortune straight off the ground," Wafer said. Wafer accused. "Nothing comes that way."

"Except for you," Stobo said resentfully. "You got that great hunk of sapphire straight off the ground, didn't you? Just like that. My God, what I'd give to pick up just a few raw lumps like that. What's so special about you, you don't have to grub away for years?"

"He is special," Emmie said matter-of-factly. And didn't look at him, as if looking away confirmed his specialness.

"I would if I could," Wafer said, trying to be agreeable.

"Would what?" Stobo asked.

"Show you. Take you there."

"Oh can't you see," Emmie asked impatiently, rising and scratching her fair hair with irritable fingers, "that what means a lot to you mightn't mean a thing to him. Not a thing."

"See what's happened to you already," I said. "Just like Doss said."

"Where's your sense of adventure, you lot?" Stobo asked. "You're so old, Emmie, horribly horribly old. Where's your sense of fantasy, anyhow? What about that?"

"Oh I've got that," she said pertly. "We've all got that. You don't understand," she went on, "anyone who isn't straight down the line like you are. You've never known.

I've had my dad all my life with his fabulous failure of a smile and his crooked blue eye. That made me old."

Contempt made her voice break. She was crumpling with the shame of her disloyalty.

She ran out of the pub parlour, through the bar and down the steps into the street.

Wafer went after her in a flash.

What'd ah do? What'd ah do? What'd ah do, doo doo doo, doo doo do?

Confession is not an art. It is a direct vomiting of then as I sit in now.

Sucking away at the pacifier of my tape deck as Ivy Anderson belts out "It don't mean a thing". Don't it?

How did I do what I did?

Move back to square one.

Through the clay-pans of memory I move with hunter Moon, searching the landscape for Wafer's reef.

Out there the landscape becomes so repetitive, hill chiming against hill, rock-crop clanging against rock-crop, tuffs with breccias, talus with scree, salt-pan with cirque, Moon, too, was sick with it. He wanted to retch landscape up. Perhaps Wafer's find had merely been a floater.

Moon had taken his van a hundred kilometres out and tried searching for Wafer's one-night camp in wide quarter-circle sweeps, working each way from the van and gradually narrowing in, remembering each time he repositioned the van to keep the invisible lake as his centre.

His arc swung from nor-west to nor-east and as he had begun at a point along a difficult back track, it was two days before he had come even halfway in.

On the third morning his food supplies were down but

rather than return he wasted half the morning setting rabbit traps and late in the afternoon he shot a rock wallaby, skinned it, butchered it and fried supper steaks by an unexpected rock pool in the bed of a dried-up creek that had forgotten its name. It was while he had been clambering about the hill-spurs that protected it that he thought at first he had come across traces of Wafer's camp, but when he climbed down to the blackened patch on the sand spit between the rocks, he saw it was nothing but flood detritus.

Dusk ate into him as he sat before his camp-fire and mosquitoes trembled in the fine dark. Around nine the last quarter of the moon lost itself behind cloud and the shadows all about him deepened and softened. He was a man used to lonelier and more dangerous places but all day long he had heard only two sounds that could connect him to a world of humans, a distant coughing truck that died as he listened and a chopper that went over running out scrubbers on the property west of him.

What is Jam doing, in Freddie Stobo's four-wheeler, perched on a spy-rise beyond that camp, not listening to Stobo's cheerful natter? I can see, as if I were Jam, the neat Moon rinse his mug, refill the billy, clean his skillet with sand, douse the fire and roll himself in his sleeping-bag like a secret. No, he would be mumbling into the dusty folds of it, no. Think of the House of the Little Deaths and he thought and Soledad Maria stroked his shoulders, his sweating neck and chest, dabbled fingers across his forehead and ran them slowly down the insides of his thighs into sudden wakefulness as their car bucketed down towards the creek bank and the headlight dazzle pinned him into his bag like a roo.

They advanced behind their flashlights. Jam told me he could see Moon scratching about for his gun which turned a lovely cold blue in the torch beams.

"Easy," Stobo called. "Easy there. It's me. Fred. Fred and Gab's brother."

The last of Moon's personal warmth escaped him like a little sigh as he crawled out of the sleeping-bag.

"What the hell!" he said. "Oh what the hell do you want?"

Stobo got busy with kind things first: thought he'd miss out on Christmas, only two days to go, thought he might have got bushed. "It's bad country out here," Fred said earnestly. He'd been gone too long. Thought he might have needed help.

"Tea?" Moon demanded surlily; and irritably he began to crumple paper and tuck twigs into a tent shape. The fire blazed like flower and behind its dancing black calyx Stobo and Jam squatted while Moon rolled himself a smoke, waiting, simply waiting to get down to business.

They looked at Moon's tensed profile, his face narrow with something, lines fine as wire dragging his mouth down into a two day beard. In flame flicker the stubble glinted red and his eyes, heavy and dark, said nothing.

"Any luck?" Stobo asked as carelessly as he could when they were at last sharing a mug of tea and Moon grunted about his failure. The other two could hardly hear his muttered comments on the land, the search, his failure to turn up even a streak of colour anywhere.

"I've been doing some thinking," Stobo said when he judged the moment right. "Some pretty pertinent thinking." He sucked at the tea easily and luxuriously while Jam waited his turn. I'm glad Jam had to wait. "I've talked to Doss about it but you know women. Tells me to mind my own business. But that's just the point. It's our business, mate. The whole town's business. I think the old girl's taken a bit of a shine to Wafer, so we won't get much go-ahead from her. But I had a word with Brim and I saw Cropper. They're all of a mind."

Moon said nothing, squatting before the fire, stirring it now and again with a stick.

"Look at it this way," Stobo half pleaded. "Wafer could be sitting on a fortune there. He doesn't know it or if he does, he doesn't care. That's more to the point, isn't it, Jam? He doesn't bloody care. Christ! I ask you! But there it is and what we've all got to do is talk some sense into him and the more there are of us who feel this way, the better. You haven't been around this place too long so you wouldn't have a clue about how the folk feel when a mining town dies on its feet. You wouldn't know. But maybe if there's a strike where he picked up that thing, maybe it could all start up again. It could do wonders for the place."

"I want wonders for me."

"Now that's selfish," Stobo said gently. Ever so gently. "This could be something for all of us. We've got to try to get that obstinate bugger to show us the exact spot, and then things can get going for everyone."

"You came to check on me," Moon said.

"Fair go, mate," Stobo lied quickly and Jam kept quiet. "That's a rotten thing to suggest."

"It's why you came," Moon said sourly. "You thought I might have struck a payload."

"You can think what you like," Stobo said. "Jerrold and I really were concerned —"

"Yes, and we know what about. Well, you can both relax, fellers. Not a trace. Not a speck. Now, will you let me get some shut-eye?"

"Look," Stobo said. "Look, it's no good fighting amongst ourselves, is it? We've got to get together on this one, like I said."

"You're wasting your time with him," Moon replied. "It doesn't mean anything to him. Not to him, a great big gasping humanitarian like that."

"Okay okay," Stobo said. He finished his tea angrily

90

and passed the mug to Jam. "But he doesn't have to be in it. He only has to show us. And like you say if he's the big humanitarian you reckon he is, then he wouldn't want to deny us, now would he?"

Moon thought about that and the silence extended just too long until Jam asked, "What about Colley? Would he be interested?"

"He's still in hospital but he's due back for Christmas," Stobo said.

"And he's another one," Moon said reflectively. Not to Stobo. Not to my brother. To space. "Another queeroh. He'd bugger up anything. It's like a gift. And who —" and Moon holds up a fifteen second pause like some discovery before he could get the question out, and leant back into darkness away from the fire —" is looking after the kid?"

Stobo leant forward after him. "I wouldn't ask that if I were you," he said. He'd only just heard the story from Jam. "She's okay. She's not such a kid. Fourteen. Fifteen. Wafer's keeping an eye on her. It's only for a couple of days. She's making out."

As if he were confronted by another lost gem-field, Moon shakes a fazed skull.

I keep seeing them bulked dark against dark around that tiny fire, now puttering out. Perhaps when Moon's gun, rigid with Puritan ferocity, had blasted a fornicator into kingdom come, it had been only a lewd punishing of himself. Stobo's probing and curious eye made him turn his discomfort away as history punished him. Not only senses. Some long-gone Caribbean ancestor scooting his privateer in and out of the narrow green islands that floated like which-way seeds on a blue tide that kept shoving his thoughts into a lush decadence he actually hated. At times his body must rear horse-wise against the imposed continence of the desert vision. Sour with mischance he said, more to the obliterated

91

horizon, than to them, "I was getting fed up, anyway. Swags of potch. Over and over."

"And what if he really can't remember?" Jam asked then. "I mean what if he really has forgotten the exact spot. It all looks pretty much the same round here, for him especially. He wouldn't have the eye for it we have. We've been here all our lives. We know the place."

"There is that," Moon said. "But he remembers. I'm certain he remembers."

"That's it," Stobo said, suddenly cheerful. "Think positive." Having taken life easy so long behind the beer-kegs of the Wowser, he could enjoy the force of causes.

Moon's abrupt rage stunned them.

He twisted around from the fire, his face shadowed but his voice brutal. "We'll make him show us. Make him. What've we got there, eh? Look at him. Some delicate-blooded reader who's come to a god-forsaken place like this drummed on by a dream he's got of finding his own fucking Eden. A two foot thick concrete sheltered Garden of Paradise. Oh God, I know. I've heard the crazy stories from Colley. Some kind of gentle nut making it for himself. He can make it for us, too, the sod. If this place is his shelter, his bloody Eden, by God I bet he remembers the portals."

That nice articulateness of fury.

Stobo was querying "portals".

"The gates," Moon said with contempt. "The moment. The precise fucking spot. He's chock-a-block with senti-ment. He'd remember all right. And he can remember for the rest of us who've been lost for a lifetime." Remembering his mammy and the poboy sandwiches and the truckies full of breeze.

Stobo became uncertain. He didn't want bullying. Basically, he was a genial man.

"I don't think getting tough with him will help. Pushing."

"It always helps."

"Not this way, mate. Not this way. Okay, so I want us all to get a share. But nice and friendly. We don't want any rough stuff. I thought if we all kept at him a bit, nagged him a little, showed him what it means to the town, a kind of sympathetic pestering, we'd wear him down. He's not such a bad bloke."

"Oh Christ!" Moon whispered. "You bloody bonehead. Why did you bother to come?"

Stobo ground out his cigarette, slowly, thoroughly and didn't bother to look up as he said,

"On Moh's scale, Moon, I reckon you'd grade the full ten."

Jam urged Stobo back to the truck. He said he kept saying, "We've done what we could. We've done what we could."

Tell me, Jam, tell me if you took a last look at Moon's black anger rising above his fire above his water-hole. It seems to me, but maybe I'm being wise after the event, that then his anger began moving out through the night as if it might engage the world.

By lamp-light, an ironic blast-back, Wafer was contemplating a daguerreotype of his grandparents.

The wretched group was posed loosely before a settler's hut, vintage late nineties, togged up in the church-wise floppy modesty of the time. Those ties! That stuffy serge! Those ground-dragging skirts! Those hats! And the heat that would have been flowing about them.

There was a pretty young woman, head bowed, standing to the left behind a felled log near which two chickens were scratching uselessly. A bucket lay on its side. The young woman was wearing a formal long-

sleeved dress and a shallow-crowned broad-brim hat
with a ribbon and she appeared to be unnaturally
interested in her hands. Behind her, the cook-house
lean-to was profiled against the water-tank and a stand
of stringy-bark. A few feet away, staring sadly at the
ghostly camera-man was a girl of seven or eight with
passionate swoops of long hair so like Emmie my heart
jumped. She stood awkwardly and obediently in front of
the post verandah with her kid brother and sister wearing shapeless hand-me-downs.

And closer to the camera, the bearded dad, shirt-
sleeved for the big deal, cradled a baby. Their moment.
Frozen. So I can gawp now, eighty years on, flapping at
the flies and stunned by their hardship, scanning the
hessian curtained annexe to the right of the group
where, just for a moment as a sullen breeze moves it, I
glimpse a table, a bucket and a large iron wash-tub.

I cannot look up at Emmie or Wafer, both breathing
gently at my shoulder, as I collapse listless in the house
with its sagging frame, its shingles. There's only the
briefest patch of grass and the crowded desolation of the
photo fills me unexpectedly with such sadness for that
long-gone family, I know oh I know the temperature
beating on their Sunday best is in the high nineties.

"That," Wafer says pointing to the baby in the calm
man's arms, "is my father."

Looking, I cannot believe that that moment is gone,
stopped, finished for ever. I believe, believed, long
before Wafer confirmed my wild theories for me, that
the psychic energies of the Monets, the Mozarts, the
Rodins are forces that keep on exploding through our
world. Soul, I call it. Now I believe it's the same for those
who aren't Mozarts or Rodins or Monets. I say as much.

No one smiles.

"And that?" Emmie's finger is touching ever so gently
the woman's arm which is, I realize now, resting lightly

above another pregnancy. Emmie is ignoring my philosophic challenge as if I'm thieving Wafer's thunder.

"My grand-mother. And that very pretty little girl, Emmie, the one rather like you, was my great-aunt Clancy."

Why should Wafer notice the likeness, I think unreasonably.

"Who was raped," he was adding unsuitably, "at fifteen and ran away from home shortly after."

"Oh." Emmie's eyes riveted on the sepia blandness of the cardboard. "Almost like me," she says.

Wafer winces but goes on. "And that, "— pointing to the next small girl — "was Aunty Looby and with her Uncle Simon (a bed-wetter of distinction). And that, Grandfather Wafer."

Emmie picked the picture up between pink-tipped thumb and forefinger, moving it closer to the light, poring over it.

"They look so alive then," she said awkwardly. She couldn't drag her eyes away from this trapped moment eighty years away.

"As if they hadn't been," she said, about to thieve my thunder.

"There's me," Wafer said.

Neither of us could cope with that.

"The sad thing," Emmie went on, "was the real of them. I mean they used to look forward to things like us, wait for Christmas. And now it's as if it never happened. I can't bear it, you know," she added seriously, turning her face away from mine as if there were no possibility I would understand and glutting on Wafer's as if he might open up the world. "It makes everything seem pointless."

She looked back again then at poor raped Aunt Clancy with her exquisite child-face gazing so wistfully at the photographer. Watch the dickey-bird, love, the big raping dickey-bird. Has he got something in store for you!

"When was it taken?"

"Have a look at the back. It will tell you. Faintly, it will tell."

The ink was the palest brown on the spotted cardboard, but still legible, the letters sweeping confidently forward into what was to be their nothing: Family and self, upper Burdekin, May, 1902.

I watched Wafer watching Emmie watching his long-dead family and wondered if his heart-muscle took the same tremendous leap as mine when Emmie's hair, swinging carelessly forward under the lamp, blurred that of Clancy, became it.

For just one pulse-stopping second I saw Wafer's hand jerk forward to touch the sloping hair; then it moved back as quickly and his fingers clenched and bit into the palm.

"You wouldn't imagine," he was saying, his voice altered with effort, "but they became quite wealthy. It might all look sad and hopeless there, Emmie," (was he ignoring me?) "but they moved on from that settler's hut, that pig, that old washing-tub and bought another property and a better. Finally they built a very flash homestead and got over Aunt Clancy — or seemed to — she was never mentioned, my father told me. Then the family moved south to even greener pastures and my grandfather sweating so quietly in his Sunday serge left almost everything to the Bedwetter. Who became hideously rich."

That silenced us. The clock's ticking was like small drums. I heard my blood take over. Or Wafer's.

And after a while Emmie said,

"You've spoiled it now, telling us that. The whole magic of an old photo like that is in the mystery, I mean not knowing. Not knowing what happened, if they got away from the hut, the scraggy old trees, whether Aunt Clancy – "

She stopped. Logically really. For her eyes had found the small light-thorn of the bus-house down by the lake and what was so different really between pioneer time then and pioneer time now?

Wafer nodded, his face grey, poking the picture back into a manila folder that bulged with mementos I wanted urgently to inspect.

This country, like St Lawrence's rack, provides terrible tensions between landscape and flesh. The strain crawled over Wafer's exhausted face; it was there in the picture of his grandparents; it was under my skin like scrub-itch. The solution is submission, father advised me in a moment of tipsy parenting. Wafer tells me too.

And in the end the landscape wins.

"Do you realize, both of you," I said aggressively, "that this nothing of a place once had two thousand people in the boom days of the mine. There were three pubs, a small bush-hospital. Oh the lot. A weekly news-sheet, a School of Arts stacked with fly-blown books. As old and spotted," I added nastily, "as that bit of family-album nostalgia."

I think he understood the reason for my malice, smiling within weathered eyes, widening them as if he wanted to take anything in, anything at all.

"The trouble," he said, "is that this country, this tough backblocks stuff, pays little tribute to elegance. Even of expression."

Checkmate.

Dark was towelling up the whole landscape and running into my pores.

"We don't reach up when the struggle's over. Or when we're bushed. We don't reach forward when we're down. We reach down even further, trying to beat the swing of the wheel."

It's easy enough to follow but I don't agree with him and then Emmie, astute Emmeline Colley, puts a sample in the nub.

"Like my dad," she says. "Oh my dad."

I have a downward mobility. Sometimes the clack phrases of the jargon makers have their own ironic antitheses.

Thinking in my insomniac bed about Wafer's last remarks, I know it is not nature that abhors a vacuum but man, the little bitzer who doesn't harmonize with space. It's the space. It grinds us all down till we're crumbs on the floor, terrified little messes that have to be swept away or burnt right out of existence.

Perhaps it is time for Wafer's bomb.

His shelter must be satiric, surely, a gesture of thumb to nose at the shonky deal life hands out. There is only one perfect shelter: indifference. Some would suggest it's confidence in the Lord. But no, I think it is complete dispassionateness about the fate of this shaky globe. Wafer, you don't have to move over for me, to make room. I'll be sitting here smiling when it comes.

Of course that was midnight bravado interlarded with an absurd envy of Emmie's youth. I think about youth. I do little sums on the biblical factor. I mentally post letters to heads of state saying dear X, on average, you have only two hundred and forty months to live, a sobering thought, yours sincerely and know I'd be arrested for threats through her majesty's mails and in this state forced to have a psychiatric examination as well. Just think about it. Think.

These days I'm pausing and thinking too much.

Have I changed sides?

This story has chased round town and Moon is its source.

I have to imagine Wafer, who has been acting as Emmie's daddy for the days in which Smiler has been away, staring from his bunk-kingdom in the morning dark of Christmas Day at the shake-down he has made for Emmie at the far end of his room. I can only squint at the blurred movie which finds Emmie, towards dawn, rolled up in a blanket on the floor beside his stretcher and Wafer, looking down, wakened by something, finding her face emptied of everything and with the mild smoothness of water like part of a dream from the shallow kind of sleep that keeps dreams afloat after waking.

Oh Emmie! That was too much immolation. I refuse to accept it as a child cowering from bogles. You are not that sort of child.

How long watching her? How long inspecting the half-sigh, the half-turn, the solvable curve of hip up-thrust against blanket, her breathing so slight it could only ripple the dawn-light flowing across the vows of self-denial pinned to the wall, the jokey placards.

He was accountable, he must have had to keep telling himself, his body and mind an unaccustomed riot of small lusts. How he must have fought it, creeping out to make tea. And then, the ticking sounds of water and primus stretching the saucepan's metal, must have woken her.

Mind you, I only had Wafer's words for all this, but when he found she was awake and watching him, he took her back a cup of tea and put it on the floor beside her.

She told him then what a father he'd make, asking was that the right word and Wafer, old stickler for the *double entendre juste,* had said he didn't think it was, quite. It was at that moment, if I care to believe in nature's theatrics or his, that the second storm of the wet broke, spitting nails of water all over the tin roof of the shack, cracking the place open with sound and splattering leaks across the floor while Emmie glumly trailed her blanket like some comic-strip bysie as Wafer sat prim on the bed edge, islanded on the driest spot in the room. He was aware of her snivelling and then he said, annoyed with the child in her, "Oh come on. Come on in."

She had stood unsurely by his bed and when he moved back for her lay down beside him shivering, but not with cold, Emmeline Colley, still wrapped in your blanket, oh not with cold.

The snuffling of which-what tears. The shivering.

Normal again he half-whispered "Christ oh Christ" and then he had taken her, wrapped as she was, into his rocking there-there arms, a jumbled mess of half-sleep, blanket and weepy complaint.

"There," he had said. "There."

As fathers do.

Stroking her hair. As fathers do. If his body responded naturally to the feel of her he ignored it, choked almost with the ache of it, and in her semi-sleep Emmie might have been aware that he put his mouth carefully and briefly against her forehead.

Wideawake, he swore, he had cradled her as he might a baby.

Maybe he concentrated on the thinness of her wrists or the scattering of freckles on her face as a counter to lust.

I believe that now, that that was the all of it. I'm certain now. But what does any of this after-knowledge mean? I couldn't have real wisdom at the age I was then, could I? At thirteen, thirty, three hundred? Wisdom isn't in this life.

Anyway, Moon found them like that.

Happy Christmas everyone.

Emmie had woken to hear Wafer's voice protesting, "You're wrong, you know."

She was alone in the bed, the rain still thudding, and outside on the verandah she could see Wafer in his sloppy toga, his unlikely lover face short-sightedly blinking at Moon's whispered "You rotten sod."

Wafer, with the impulse to flippancy that always caught him in the epicenter of calamity had replied:

"Oh it's a matter of aesthetics with you, is it? My unappetizing self!"

Moon had swung at him then and Wafer rubbed the cracked side of his head, the throb spreading inside his skull as he saw Moon's arm pulled back again for a second punch. He dodged back protesting "You'll wake her." His head felt like a thickly aching tooth. "You wouldn't want to wake her, would you? Not you."

Moon dropped his arm. "And what does that mean?"

"You know what it means. Emmie told me about you. About the day at the water-hole. I don't have to detail it for you, do I?"

"Lies."

"I believed her. I still believe her."

"Fantasy," Moon said sourly. "Hogwash. And you can prove nothing. But this is something different. Oh God yes, it's different. The whole town will hear about this. They'll run you out, man. They've been waiting for an excuse and now you've given it to them."

Moon's face was heavy with the river, the grove, a lifetime of unrelenting guilt.

"It's only your word against mine," Wafer said.

"She's been living here."

"Ridiculous," Wafer said. "Ridiculous. You're ruining, you have ruined, things for Emmie for no reason. Think of her father. He'll be back tomorrow."

"Amigo," Moon said unpleasantly, "he'll be the first to know."

The grubby Santas, the patchy synthetic snow in the Allbut store, the box of unsold Christmas cards brought out each year and whose quantity never ˙seemed to diminish: the town was lying discarded in the heat and rain of its own Bethlehem.

I see Moon, his eyes with the opacity of stone, see his muscles leap along the spring of his bare thighs as he grasps the verandah rail, poised and paused in a threat curved above Wafer, his hands grasping because they might have struck again and again this poor crud who'd beaten him to it, beaten him to what he'd resisted for weeks with a puritan fire that ate him out until that uncontrolled moment at the water-hole. The House of the Little Deaths had enforced a frightful penance of celibate repugnance.

Emmie slid out of bed, her face staring from a mass of uncombed hair. The men weren't expecting this but she glared at and through them as if she might solve them both.

"You do that," she threatened Moon, her face chalky, "you do just that and I'll kill you."

She held the men's eyes.

And then while they stared back, mockingly she dragged her night-gown over her head, stood there with her still forming body, small girl adult, and ridiculed them both with her nudity.

Emmeline, how could anyone cope with a child like you?

Routed they had watched her stalk her naked scorn

103

down the hill across the sodden paddock under rain to
her father's house.

Brim, the town-clerk, was trying his empire-builder's face on Wafer and its beam shone earnestly from features whose seriousness had been dissipated by too many quick deals, too many grogs. He sported a spade-like beard of intense red and was given to pith helmets and bush shirts. Sitting behind his old-fashioned desk he could have been stuck on an out-back station in the veld; but he was here, a someone in Allbut.

His "Spare a minute?" had trapped Wafer outside the store and now Wafer sat opposite seeing Brim's plump liver-spotted hands shovelling papers around on the desk, the living symbol of a country martyr who must be suckled in his martyrdom so that his condition might be finally bearable. Rimless glasses kept sliding down the fleshy bridge of his nose and he would peer over them while he spread his bulk in the chair and waited for Wafer's reply.

Deliberately Wafer dangled his head on one side and looked helpless, irritating Brim who kept shoving his argument along.

"You must see," he said, "from what I'm told this could be the big thing the town's been waiting for. I've watch-ed it go down over the last fifteen years till it's almost nothing. Rebirth." He liked the sound of the word. "A renewed interest from the outside. Maybe a plug of foreign capital. It's happening everywhere else in the state. Why not here? It's exactly what this town needs. You must see that, surely?"

Wafer's silence was absorbing a small quiver he had observed starting in the fleshier parts of the other man's cheeks.

"You see," Councillor Brim continued not so patiently, "I don't believe, in fact no one believes for a moment, that you can't remember. I'm sure you do. No one could pick up a piece of gemstone like that and not remember. I could understand you not wanting to disclose the place if you wanted to stake out a claim for yourself. But you don't, do you?"

Even using the word "claim" made Brim feel he'd struck it rich. He smiled. His teeth were small and spaced.

"Then don't you think your attitude is really dog-in-the-mangerish?"

"No."

"Good God, man!" Brim cried, losing control, his gut shaking as he leant forward over his desk as if to inspect. "There's no reason to you, is there?"

"There's plenty of that." I can hear Wafer say it, setting his face stubbornly to the light from the window behind Brim's chair. "There might be nothing worth mining at all. If an outsider like me, an uninterested outsider like me, could stumble on it, then anyone round here with ten times the knowledge of the place could do the same."

"You've put your tongue on the right word there," Brim said, exasperated into maliciousness. "Outsider. This town doesn't owe you anything. We've been pretty decent to you, though. Helping when we could. You owe us. What's the big reason for being here, anyway?"

'I like it. I simply like it."

"Don't get too fond," Brim warned. "We could rescind your lease, you know. We don't need trouble makers."

"'Trouble?"

"There was that business with the circus. You went right against the town's wishes in that matter. You're too friendly with the boongs. And now there's something else."

"What else?"

"Old Colley's daughter. There's a nasty story going round the town. You don't want to get our backs up. Not if you want to hang on to that lease."

Brim told everyone later that the maddening mildness with which Wafer agreed was almost more than he could bear.

"I won't fight you on that," Wafer said. "I'm not a fighter, can't you see? I simply want to be."

Now I see it. Now. Too late. The simplicity of his needs was what, after all, made his life difficult. The rest of us craved complexity. His meekness was constant reproof.

Let me paint in some more fragments of his personal life I'd scrapped together. There had been a woman once, a married woman, and I become part of those long sunny afternoons, the rumpled bed, the pressed grass. That was all there was to it, he swore: the moment. The laughter before or even during, memories of small upstairs cafes, rocky coves along the coast, outdoor tables and the waiter asking "Will there be anything else?" No, Wafer would say. No. I don't think there will be and Ruth (that was her name) had always kept her smile even, on her beautiful face, and once, only once, had said with the plea of a question in her words straight after he had said no there wouldn't be anything else, "I want to leave him." And he had said, "But this is enough, surely?" Too late to seize that moment by its silky blonde forelock. Too late to tug it gently lifting that remembered calm of hers into a surprise of delight.

Wafer had sighed, remembering. Perhaps Brim thought the sigh was for him.

"Think about it, about what I've said," he suggested. "They all know out there. All of them. There's a certain feeling about. People resent. They feel they're being denied. Resentment. You know how it is."

Wafer knew.

I knew, too.

After all, he had carried with him all his life that tatty baggage that bred resentment in others wherever he went. He needed nothing but himself. I see there the blueprint for my own early years, the wanting of others who in the long run gave nothing you couldn't supply yourself or didn't tire of. He hated himself for his completeness. The wounded man looked up again on the trail back from Nam Dinh, his eyes glinting in jungle-light, and said, "Jesus, fancy being saved by a shit-house bastard like you." Wafer had continued phlegmatically strapping the wounded man on to a stretcher and then administered a pain-killer, all in silence, until the outrageous resentment on the sergeant's face blanked out and he perceived only the open-mouthed snarl of the hideous wound in the sergeant's chest which, though plugged with pads, continued to ooze rancour.

But you've never mentioned it before, I had said, being in the army. Father *would* be pleased. Not a real soldier, he had said. A stretcher bearer in the medical corps. There was no where else they could put me. Or Ruth, I had asked. Tell me more about Ruth.

You need me now or then or later or some time, she had said to him as the funky blues pianist played late-night music around the empty bottles, the garlic bread baskets. But not after now, she had continued, or before then or earlier than later. And for the tiniest moment her mouth puckered with grievance that she managed to smile away with the empty bottles, the dirtied ash-trays.

108

"I wish it weren't like that," he had admitted, reaching across and correcting the pucker with the gentlest finger-tip.

It was then she struck him.

They could have been his last words to her and he had felt impelled to utter them again knowing there never was absolution.

As I know.

Ruth, wherever you are, I have struck too. But finally.

"I know," Wafer had said to Councillor Brim.

"Then you will think about it?"

"I didn't say that."

How could Councillor Brim, too, refrain from striking? I see all his features crowd together as he frowns.

"Just a bit of friendly advice," he said with great effort. "No one minds a bit of friendly advice, do they?"

Wafer followed him into the street steaming from the last rain-fall and looked down the road to where the monument stuck up from the grass and the stumpies. Even from where he stood he could read the graffito.

"Thank you," he heard himself saying. "It's a — it's a caring town."

Moon was picking out a meditative tune on the crippled pub piano, slow, thoughtful, tricky.

His hands moved with an unconcern that made it seem too easy; and no one was listening anyway except Stobo who kept coming over to watch between serves. It was to be a prelude, though Moon didn't fully know that yet, sensing mainly through his fingers which kept searching out the most unusual of minor chords. He had a gift. It was a clever trick the way he could make respectable sounds come out of the most beaten up instrument.

"How's about some Christmas tunes?" Stobo asked, one day too late.

Moon sang in Spanish:
la muerte
entra y sale
de la taberna.

He might be singing the words past Stobo, as we watch, past Doss swinging the beer pumps, through the half dozen drinkers at the end tables, but Soledad Maria was crooning for him among the geraniums outside the crumbling house in Rua Gaspar Viana; over the crushed herbal scent of geranium leaves came the riper shouts of fish and melon, the rotting odour of sapodillas stacked in a basket by the door. And the harbour waters, sluggish under summer.

Moon shut his eyes against Stobo's open mouth holding its question like a plum. Under his fingers the piano lamented along with his voice and closed out for the moment rain-pitted roads of Allbut, the nervous metal of tin roofs, the outskirt humpies, the monument, the disc of the lake; and the river swung right through his arteries pumping its slow past into this present.

Stobo was about to turn away when Moon reached over with one hand and pulled at his shirt.

"Death," he said, "goes in and out of the tavern. In and out, out and in of the tavern."

"What's that, mate?" Stobo asked, his head to one side like a bird's.

Moon didn't bother to look at him and, almost intoning, he changed the melody on the cracked keys and chanted, "Oh how hard to love you as I do. Loving you makes the air, my heart and my hat hurt."

"Not with you, cock," Stobo said grinning.

Moon's eyes snapped into present tense. "The words. You asked me."

Both hands went back to crawling across the keyboard like a lover's. Ah shit, Stobo said softly, moving off with his tray and smacking down the drinks for Sergeant Cropper and Brim. The place was starting to crowd up, three of the abos blind as bats on the verandah, Headmaster Rider and my father gently molo on whisky and quarrelling over a game of euchre. There was a bunch of cowhands in spending Christmas pay and I heard Stobo murmur to Doss as he passed her behind the bar:

"Christ, that Moon. I've got a feeling it's going to be a rough old night."

Doss brushed back some damp hair that kept trailing her round flushed forehead. "Do me a favour, Freddie. Just keep it moving."

"I don't like it, somehow."

"Don't like it? Don't like what?"

"Something's different. There's a different feel."

"Heat, dear," she said. "And what will yours be, Joe?"

Gawd, Stobo thought as Doss joked "No, you can't have me, love. So what will it be instead, eh?" Great roar of laughter what a card! And it's the women who are supposed to have the intuition. He mopped the bar top down automatically and I saw him stop in the middle of it to speculate on Moon's stooped shoulders as he played the same tune over and over, his singing lost in the cage babble of the drinkers.

By eight the room was jammed and the din cracked the swinging-doors apart on a shamble of beer-gut and singlet spilled out to drink on the verandah, bodies oblique in drinker's stance, buttock out-thrust, hand on rail.

All under the unsteady light from the generator as it blinked on and off, faded and flared.

By nine Moon had left the piano and was sitting tense in a corner, smoking endlessly and puddling a sort of finger-map in the beer slops on the table.

I am waiting for Wafer.

I am starting to hate Wafer.

Why?

He is out there now ferrying back Emmeline and her wounded Dad like the great little Samaritan that he is from the hospital at Mainchance. He has given up his whole day to playing not quite fathers.

I am waiting under the arhythmic thunk of the dart-board and the crash of glasses.

At nine-thirty I hear, just hear, his van grind up outside the pub and within minutes Wafer's gentle and solemn face is poking through the barrier of racket.

Even he who tries never to be surprised was surprised by the dropping silence as if gerry-built walls of noise had collapsed all over the room and through this quiet

112

ne duck-footed it to the bar where Stobo, catching Doss's warning eyes, spread his hands along the bar edge and leaned forward in what became a parody of minehost.

"And what will it be, mate?" Stobo asked.

The whole room was listening.

"A dozen soft," Wafer said unblushing.

Someone laughed.

"How's the old boy, then? Aren't you going to bring him in for a bit of a cheer-up?"

Moon was watching Wafer and Moon was coiled in an angry spring.

Brim seemed to have frozen with a schooner half way to his lips. Cropper stood up and kept easing his trousers, doing little knee-bends.

"He's not with me."

"Not with you mate?"

Doss bustled down the bar, her rigid hair-set starting to fall apart in the humidity.

"What do you mean, lovey, not with you? Wasn't he supposed to be discharged today?"

Stobo kept stacking Wafer's order impassively as if he hardly dared look up.

"They're keeping him another week," Wafer said. "He's developed a clot."

"Bugger of a trip, lovey," Doss said, "for nothing." The brassy nimbus of her hair was directed like a flare, challenging any drinker to speak. "Where's the kid, then? She must be disappointed."

Wafer's mouth tightened. "Out in the car. We're just on our way home."

"Poor kid," Doss said. "What a way to spend a day like this bucking through the heat to Mainchance. Why don't you bring her in and we'll put her up for the night. No trouble at all."

"She wants to go home."

"Oh come on, lovey," Doss coaxed as the room hung on

her wheedling. "It's too lonely out there. Bring her in and I'll make up a bed for her. It's no fun stuck out there with only you old codgers nosing about. What she needs is a dream-boat like Fred here, eh Fred?"

"That's right, mate," Stobo grinned engagingly all of a sudden. "Like Doss says, like me. What's the hurry, anyway? Stay and have a drink. Young Rider's here and Em and he can play darts or listen to the radio out the back. They're still playing carols," he added, and burst into song: " 'Oh come all ye faithful, drink up at the Wowser!' "

The men laughed and started adding lines and in the middle of it Wafer picked up his carton and started obstinately for the doors saying, "Thanks all the same Fred. Thanks Doss. But we're both bushed."

Things got funny then.

When he reached the swing doors he discovered that the men who had been around the bar somehow were in front of him, were crowding him as he tried to push through. Father shuffled his cards together and was watching with the curious joy of a pedant, the squarest grammarian of orthodoxy observing an oddball ride for a fall.

"Death or bane," Wafer murmured predictably but meaninglessly to the half dozen faces confronting him. They were strangers, part of the stockman pack. And then he caught my eye.

No wonder father was smiling. Flummox them with a quote, the old boy had always advised me, displaying the cagey side of an erudition I had never suspected. If you get into a corner, he had said, that will fix them. And he must have been on to something for the bar room mob were temporarily stayed. You could almost feel the air ripple as they put their mental brakes on.

Wafer saw me, smiled quizzically and then there was movement, a kind of surge back by the swing doors and

I heard Emmie's voice, clear and brief in the hot night, the slam of the van door.

Sergeant Cropper ceased his little leg dance, pushed out through the men and in a minute he was back again urging Emmie into the room ahead of him.

"I think you ought to stay," Sergeant Cropper said to Wafer. "We've all missed you."

The sergeant was full of menace with a familar protective arm about Emmie's shoulders. "Em won't mind waiting a bit, will you, love? How was the dad, Em? Tell us how the dad was."

To my unadoring eyes Emmie seemed older.

At first she had appeared like an animal startled in car headlights but as she slowly glanced all round this crowded arena, I could see her poise firming even when she caught my eye, Jam's, Timothy Rider's besotted grin, even when I saw her add Moon's shadowy presence to her total, his face shiftingly distorted by the fizz of a match.

Emmie gazed back at me calmly, back into my forced encouraging smile, dismissed me, looked at Wafer and knew they both were at bay.

"My father is much better, thank you, Sergeant Cropper," she said bunging on her private school accent. "He'll be home in a week."

"Not before time, eh?"

Cropper could make anything sound knowing. He was born to nourish feelings of guilt. After all, it was tremendous sport for a bloke stuck here in the arse-hole of the state. The only sport. Some expert bullying round and about, flashing rank for doing without the side-kicks and perks that came the way of colleagues in the cities. How he must have pined for the massage parlours of Brisbane so that he could offer a little protection. But he made up for it, not in money but a squandering of his soul in violence of the spirit, always backing his leer with a raging lawfulness that he believed to be part of the job. Or pretended to believe. He might ride a gin now and again when he was away on scrub duty or even in the back room closenesses of the shanties but that didn't, by God, stop him from chasing the drunken sows off main street and shoving them in the lock-up for a night's cool-off without benefit of chamber pot. Sitting in their own piss. Watching coldly next morning as they swilled the cell down.

"You run along with Doss," Sergeant Cropper ordered, ignoring the accent and flattening his own, "because Mr Wafer's staying for a little drink with the boys."

Emmie turned slowly to face him.

"I prefer to go home."

"Well, now," Cropper said, "that's a bit mean, isn't it? Didn't think you were a mean girl, Emmie. Thought you were a real generous girl. This kind man's been nice enough to drive you all the way to see your old dad and you don't even want to stop while he has a little drink."

"I'm sure he doesn't want a little drink."

Sergeant Cropper's hand became quite painful on her upper arm.

"Now how can you be sure of that, eh? How can you be so sure? You don't know everything, girlie."

She kept straightening and smoothing the front of her washed-out dress with her free hand.

"It is illegal for me to be in this bar, Sergeant Cropper," she said.

Father roared with laughter and a snigger spread around the room.

"And you are detaining me," she continued, plucking with exaggerated fastidiousness at the restraining fingers. Uselessly.

"Oh quite the little lawyer, Em," Sergeant Cropper said, grinning. "But we don't want to detain you. Doss!" he roared suddenly. "Doss come and get this kid and take her out the back where it's not illegal. Now listen, missie, I'm telling you. Just you sit tight till this kind bloke has his little drink with all his mates. That's all we're asking."

Emmie looked across at Wafer who gave the most fractional of nods.

"All right," she said finally, "but I'll wait in the car."

The laughter died. Doss, full of spleen, swung out from behind the bar.

"Hands off that kid, Cropper," she ordered, "or she'll be filing a suit for assault as well. Come along, lovey. All men know is bully. Bully and shout. Part of the same thing, really. The louder it's said the more important. If you'd worked in a pub, dear, you'd never say women yakked again."

"I don't really want to stay, Doss," Emmie complained. Her voice broke a little after her brief stand and I could see, we all could, that she was tired to the bone and only two breaths from kid-yowls.

"Now now," Doss soothed. "Now you come along out the back till the sergeant calms down. The car's no place to wait out there in the dark. He's paranoid, love, and both you and I know what that means, even if no one else here does."

She turned her impudent challenging eyes on the whole room.

"He's got to have his little way otherwise he gets even more unpleasant than nature made him and God knows that's some."

Emmie allowed herself to be led out to the kitchen and I saw Timothy Rider put down his handful of darts and follow.

Wafer's face retained an unassuming blankness that refused to see anyone, even me, and after a minute I slipped out the front of the pub and went round the side to the back just in time to hear Doss say, "They don't mean anything by it, lovey. Not anything that makes sense or reason. They're just doing their male stuff, pardon Tim, having to be cock of the walk. The old bravissimo gene working overtime. My God, what a laugh."

Emmie smiled at that. She was still smiling when I slid round the door and stood awkwardly looking at the three of them.

"You stupid kids," Doss was saying affectionately. "Get yourselves comfortable and I'll make you a cuppa. Prince Fred can hold the bar."

"Let me," I said.

Looking back, that was the only decent thing I did in the whole business. The smallest gesture.

And for a while we were all smiling at each other after Emmie had had a little weep and Timothy Rider held one of her hands and looked coltish. Emmie's smile was curly, like the old Smiler's.

Inside, in that rangy pub kitchen, for a while we felt secure.

Out there, a world in which the smoothed out and extended lines of Colley's smile became reassuring because of its stupidity.

The men had formed a circle, only part of which was lit by the fog-light over the pub verandah.

The rain had stopped and the smell of wet earth must have smelt the same at Nazareth. Christmas day was well over.

In the middle of the ring, Cropper and Moon stripped to their jockey shorts, bullock-horns strapped to their foreheads, feinted and lunged as they crawled round the roadway on all fours to the mocking shouts of the men. A long-winded scribble of blood ran down Cropper's left arm, dribbling post-scripts as he crawled, spotting black in the lighter patches of dirt. Moon was achieving surprising sideways leaps, pushing off with one arm, while the men roared. "Let him have it, mate! Give it to him!" None of them really liked Cropper. "Bring him down!"

"Now this is true local history," father whispered to Jam and me, and although I felt embarrassed for him and repelled by what was happening in the ring I began to feel a horrible excitement.

"Time!" Brim called, important with a stop-watch, and the two men stood up, brushed themselves off and headed back to their corners where someone had wet towels waiting. Moon adjusted his cumbersome knee-pads, took a gulp from the beer bottle he was handed and poured the rest of it over his head. They all loved that.

"Pisshead!" came a pally lout-cry from the back of the mob and the laughter had an animal yowl to it.

"Time!" Brim shouted and down they went again, scuffling with their heads and horns raised to the centre of this horrid joke.

"They've been doing this, off and on, in this town," father gabbled under the whack of the barracking, "for nearly fifty years."

How did I not know? Is there some loathsome male freemasonry about the insane ritual? Is my presence cracking a taboo?

"Why?" I ask. "For heavens sake why?"

"I believe," father replies excitedly, — "oh God! Look at that, will you? — that it all started during the Depression. Home-made entertainment. Chance of a bet."

"I hate it."

"Of course you do," father said. "Of course. Women usually aren't in on this. Not even your mother knew. If I had any authority over you, I'd pack you off — oh God, look!"

Moon had his head down somewhere near Belem and was shoving and hooking into Carib darkness that split apart as Cropper screamed.

One of Moon's horns had caught him under the armpit and ripped up into the shoulder. There was a mess of oily blood.

Moon bounced over him, straddling, waving his arms, his horns tossing, I swear, tossing, as he screamed "cornada!", face blank with victory as he stared into, through, and beyond the lot of us.

"This," said my dad, unexpectedly, and leaning close, "has great *duende*."

Moon rose slowly to his feet as Cropper hauled himself away and began mopping at the wound. Brim and Stobo dragged the sergeant over to the steps and I could hear Doss saying urgently something about ringing for the ambulance from Mainchance.

"Not yet," Cropper told her gasping. "Not yet. It's nothing. Give us just one hour."

He looked crazed. Doss began pouring iodine straight into a slash whose gaping lips roared for stitching. Cropper screamed again as the disinfectant hit him and writhed around cursing. In the shifting dark I looked over at Wafer who appeared to be trapped between two stockmen from the property beyond ours. His face was like a print on bone, ashen and hollowed, his mouth closed tight against the obscenity about him.

Since the ritual had begun he had stood there, limp between his guards — I say guards now — in front of Stobo who was still pulsing from the bull-play. Wafer's trembling registered on my canvas from scalp to thigh.

"I've had enough," I heard Wafer say softly to Stobo.

Stobo didn't hear.

Wafer made to back away and then I felt Emmie move in beside me, dragging a horrified young Rider whose face had yellowed as if he were going to be sick; and when Emmie whispered "They're mad, mad," my father seemed to come to his senses.

"Hold hard," he said. "I think it's time you kids pushed off."

Truculently Emmie said, "I'm staying." There was nothing Timothy could do.

"Why, is there more?" I whispered to father. "Worse?"

He didn't get time to answer for the men had parted again to form a natural pathway leading up to Cropper who was squatting like a bandaged soapstone idol on the steps.

"Okay," Cropper was croaking. "Okay everybody. It's winner's challenge." Maybe his wound wasn't as serious as I had thought for he managed a sort of smirk as Doss strapped pads and bandages into place. "All right,

Moon," he instructed. "Get out there, man. It's your challenge. You're new to our little rules."

"Is this −" Wafer was picking his words with caution and addressing them to space − "a town custom?"

Brim swung round on him from the top of the steps, peering over his glasses.

"Every couple of years, mate. Depends on the temper of the town. Haven't had one for three or four years now, but we've been doing it as long as I can remember just before New Year."

"But what for?"

"Don't ask bloody stupid questions. What for! Who knows what for. It amuses the boys. It's our town's special little thing. Tradition, that's what it is. Every town likes its little bit of tradition. Have something to mark it out. And this is ours."

"But the man's badly hurt."

"Don't waste your dribble tears on me, pal," Cropper said viciously. "This is a bit of prestige, see. Honourable scars. You −" He broke off, his eyes on Moon who had taken up the horns again from the step beside Cropper and was loping now, springily, with a dancer's step, around the inside of the reforming circle. "Wait for it. Now we're going to see something, eh Wafer? Winner's right. He has the right to challenge. Anybody. Anybody at all."

The threat was in italics.

I said angrily to Jam who was standing po-faced and stupid beside father, "Did you know about this?"

His eyes slid sideways at me. "Of course," he said. "Shut up now and watch."

Round and round the circle Moon cantered the men into silence, the horns on his head gleaming, the other set held out before him thrusting their curved points at the crowd. Then he began to move more slowly so that the canter became a slow prance, glancing hard now at

122

each man as he passed, easier and easier until all that could be heard was the pad pad of Moon's bare feet in the soft dust.

The circle drew back, spread out.

One of the stockmen hooked his arm through Wafer's from behind, holding him there and the other moved in on him like a wedge. Each time Moon passed him Wafer's eyes met his and I sensed a smile behind the bull's blank gaze, knew the end of all this.

The fifth time round, Moon, as if drugged by an inner source, paused in front of Wafer, swayed, blinked his eyes into watchfulness and leaned forward like a dancer on the balls of his feet.

All about, the hot night dampered sly grins and whispers.

Moon smiled. The silence swelled like a ripening fruit.

Leaning forward from the hips, heels firm on the ground, with all the grace of a torero, Moon placed the points of the horns with measured gentleness against Wafer's chest.

"You," he said.

Bookish Wafer looked, just for the moment, scared to his deepest gut.

Micro flashes of arena, the stench of lion's breath, sand and an imperial thumb down against this century's doubled up-jerked fingers, cracked across my brain with the speed of light. Moon's eyes, glinting even in the semi-dark, were empty of statements and in a minute one of the stockmen had ripped Wafer's shirt from him, dragged down his jeans and was ramming the head-gear on, strapping it into place, and shoving him forward into the circle.

"Stand still, mate," the other stockman said. Busily he bound the pads to Wafer's knees then gave him a little push. "Out you go, matey."

The verandah light threw his long-antlered shadow

grotesquely across the scuffed dirt, across the waiting faces of the group, across me, across Emmie. Someone behind him snickered and Wafer swung about, awkward and monstrous in his bull gear but read only expectancy.

"Down!" cried the time-keeper.

And despite himself, a minuscule hesitation that must have told the sense of him to resist, Wafer dropped to his knees with Moon opposite leaning forward, Moon, on all fours, his mouth in a rictus grin below the horns as if this were all normal, a party game, a funfiller.

Oh the lewdness of that wait!

"Toro!"

Moon's hissed whisper haunted the half-lit circle.

"Huh, toro!"

And then he lumbered forward, swinging heavily from side to side in a mocking parody of a bull, trotting out to one side of Wafer then darting in with his head low. The sharp tip of a horn scored Wafer's upper arm like scarlet silk and Wafer lurched away to fall on his face in the dust. When he righted himself, there was Moon waiting amid the shouts, pawing the air with his hands, pawing the dust, taurine-comic, his mouth snorting open.

There were great belches of laughter.

While Wafer knelt there, dizzy more from the idiocy of it, he swayed but dug for strategy. Hannibal, Pizarro, Wellington were his on-paper despised men but whenever had the little Corporal been dumped in a make-shift bull-ring with a set of stage-prop horns strapped to his forehead, pads to his knees?

The cuckold symbolism of their crazy heads could have been excessively funny and for the flash-second that image took, a nervous laughter shook my body, a mirth close to hysteric tears, and even in that second I saw Moon's face change and he made a second charge at

Wafer, barely giving the other man time to throw himself sideways.

They grappled furiously in the dirt, horns locking, then jerking apart, slipping askew. Who, me? Wafer's inner man must have been protesting. Why me? Why here? How?

Moon drew back and rose to a crouch position; then he butted his head forward savagely until the horns locked once more and deeply, the bases of both sets caught so closely their skulls clashed. Moon gave bull-neck sways, swinging his head strongly from side to side, trying to wrest the head-gear off Wafer. Straining. Prising.

There aren't any rules at all, I thought, watching as the slowly lifting body of Moon forced the other deliberately up and up until they were half standing and I feared Wafer's neck might snap from the ferocious thrusts it was taking, left, right, forward, back. As far as he could, Wafer let his head ride with the pagan movement, went limp and hung from Moon's tusks like a rag. Their hands had been gripping and sliding a sweaty skidway down each other's forearms but this pressure stop pitched Moon forward across Wafer's out-thrust leg. The moment Moon thudded down, face slapping into the dirt, a great cry of "Foul!" went up. "Show the bastard!" Cropper roared.

And then Brim called "Time!"

The two men edged back to the fringe of the circle, dusting themselves off, their eyes rolling stripily, flickering over each other, over us.

"This is mad stuff," Wafer was heard to say and Emmie tugged at my father's arm pleading, "Can't you stop them? Can't you?" even as the impersonal circle shoved them forward again and on the signal both men dropped to their hands and knees and scuttled to within snuffling distance.

Moon was licking at his lips busily, skinning off dust. Or something. Wafer's eyes never left his. Below the yells and urgings he managed to say "Why?"

Moon grinned and the grin didn't quite fit. Then he lowered his horns and lunged.

There was a rip of agony across Wafer's chest and when he rolled back from the hooking bone, a rosy banderole blossomed above his thumping heart.

"You're insane!" he panted and convulsed frantically again as Moon drove in, horns spiking and tearing. Half a dozen parts of back and shoulders shrilled with pain the crowd dribbled in, and through it all, through the scuffling, the insistent prodding and jabbing of that crazed and smiling head, I heard Doss Campion's voice screeching above the roar of the men, "Keep your head down, damn you. Keep it down, you fool. Oh lovey."

And when I looked at her handsome old hard-boiled face, I stopped wondering if the words were for Moon. She was slopping tears and had rushed into the ring to drag at Moon's busy heels, trying to force him off Wafer; but Brim strong-armed her back.

Wafer scrambled backwards on all fours.

Perhaps he was trying to think himself bull as if there were abstract solutions to his physical dilemma but again Moon had upstaged him and was pawing the ground, stirring up hoof-fuls of symbolic dust to the laughter of the watching men. Wafer's white dirt-streaked face stared all round the circle, his eyes blinking as they fell on Emmie pulling forward between father and me as if she had been startled from sleep and a nightmare had translated itself into this oily Lammas dark.

I tell myself now that Wafer's eyes held nothing beyond the madness of his plight. I tell myself that now. But there was a pleading sense somewhere beyond Emmie, too, and I became aware of father trembling at his own reactions. "Oh Jesus!" I heard him mutter over and over.

Wafer tore his eyes away from the three of us then, looked down into the dirt and began shifting slowly back and forth, a monstrous beast of burden.

Moon circumscribed him in small sideways jumps.

"Oh get in there!" screamed recovered Cropper, who was swallowing and laughing. "Oh get in there, you two. Show us some action! Bit of action, eh?"

The two men were now only a few feet apart. Moon kept toying with his opponent, threatening with a rush, retreating, swooping in again, tossing his horns and hooking them with each thrust.

Wafer kept his head down. There were only dribbles of blood and dirt.

His aching world became Moon's knee-pads and the tensions in Moon's legs, that muscle-force that shot like a fuse along the naked limbs down to the propped toes which had dug themselves into the earth as if it were a starting-block.

He looked up.

Instantly Moon launched himself forward.

There was a dreadful concussion as their heads, horns, shoulders crashed together and in the middle of it Wafer, pillowed on the excited roars all about him, fell backwards to find himself straddled by Moon who, with head lowered and sweeping, made the most delicate cuts across neck and throat. At first they were no more than a satiny gesture. The little crowd was shouting itself hoarse but beside me Emmie became ominously dumb.

Wafer lay there, unable to move, frightened to swing his head aside while it became obvious as we watched that with every side and back sweep Moon was gradually increasing the pressure upon the tip of the horns.

There was blood now, running steadily and despairingly, down Wafer's chest and ribs making an ever-widening lattice.

Moon had him so solidly pinned beneath him, the thighs as unrelenting as a lover's, hands bearing down on his arms just above the elbows, the full weight of him hulked on his belly, that he could not move an inch. As Wafer lay there beneath the pendulum stroke, Emmie began to shrill again and again, "let him up" and perhaps he guessed there were tears for him out here. I could see the tears for myself and hated Wafer on their account even as father began to shove forward (at last! father, at last!) protesting.

But the men were too excited to listen to anything except their own animal baying and after a sixth kiss-like sweep of the horn-tips, Moon raised his blank unquesting face to them. What timing! What a sense of dramatic shape! I can see you, Moon, still. I see you now, the sweat glistening on your body, the other figure tensed below yours in almost copulatory position.

Moon waited, swung his head slightly.

The noise dropped away, last words falling like dust into dust.

"You'd better tell us, mate," Councillor Brim said into the silence. He was munching a nervous laugh. "You'd better show us, hadn't you?"

(What is this, I ask. Show what?)

Wafer lay still in the steady babble of his blood.

Show what? his lips were shaping. Tell what?

He opened his eyes and found the steady grey gaze of Moon upon him.

"What?" he asked. "What do you want?"

Moon paused as if seeming to search for the right answer. His absurd horn-crowned head swept arcs across the night sky. Then he bent forward so that his face dripped with shadow and Wafer could see only the terrible points approach his neck.

128

They touched him lightly, the merest tip, then began to prick inwards.

"Tell me." Wafer was beginning to gabble. "Tell me for God's sake."

"The sapphire," Moon whispered — but still we heard. "Your luck. Make it work now. They want to know where you found it."

Wafer held himself still. One tusk punctured the flesh at the side of his neck. "I've told you," he replied. "I don't know."

"You know," Moon whispered. "Oh you know." Then he roared like a bull, swinging his head up again. "Tell them!"

Wafer was mumbling.

"Come on!" Moon cried. "Louder!"

Wafer was hauling his thoughts together. I knew he didn't know.

"Yes!" he shouted back suddenly. "I'll show you bastards. Yes yes yes."

I saw Moon close his eyes, the face blindly raised to sky again, and he began to edge back down Wafer's body, back off the groin, the thighs, forcing Wafer's legs apart until he was kneeling between them, his hands clamped heavily just above the knees.

Somewhere, embroidering father's weak protesting gasps, Doss began a high-pitched squawk.

Moon's face, we saw, as Wafer struggled to push his body up and away, was transfigured with zeal, his lips opening and closing as he inwardly tried out the words he felt he had to say.

"And this," he got out finally and so clearly it fed the yearning group, "is for Emmie," and the points swept down abruptly and viciously into Wafer's groin.

Wafer screamed as one of the points ripped into the inside of his thigh. He writhed furiously as the head raised itself for a second swing but in that moment of terror and confusion, Stobo had flung himself heavily from the side onto Moon and the two men rolled, grappling in the dirt, the sounds of horns cracking and through it all Sergeant Cropper's voice saying blandly,

"No dirty fighting, lad. None of that, eh?" and he had limped forward and put one huge foot on the back of the crazy Moon.

"Come on now," he said, giving a little kick and wincing from the pain under his arm, "Come on. Simmer down. Certain things are sacred." He waited for the laughter. "Fight's over, mate." Then he kicked Moon's backside hard.

Moon might have been numbed the way he kept scrabbling with Stobo, his headgear fallen to one side, knee-pads round his ankles.

So Cropper walked carefully round the two men and seemed to be measuring up for a goal. He kicked and kicked again with his heavy blunt-toed boots.

The thuds seemed to find bone.

"Up!" Cropper ordered Moon. He'd got in some nicely placed thumps for his own wound. "Up mate! My God! That was a lousy rotten thing you tried to do."

"The old crown jewels," Jam whispered. "They ought to be on the national emblem along with the beer can."

"Oh you sod," I said. "You rotten sod."

Stobo had lugged Wafer to the verandah and across into the ladies' parlour. The crowd broke up, a few hard drops of rain began smacking down and the men drifted back to the bar.

I went in and found Doss bent over the unsprung settee on which Wafer lay beginning to cut away the torn mess of undershort and blood, gasping with disgust at the smiling flesh on the inside of his leg.

And Emmie was behind me, not weeping as I might have expected, her small face set in adult mould, looking down at the steady pumping of the blood.

Doss barely turned her head as she organized and bullied helpers.

But Emmie sturdily stood her ground while I wrestled with the old hand-phone.

She stood there staring as Doss packed torn sheet strips into the hole, wad after wad, and her eyes were wide and strangely calm.

"That's a new one," I heard her say, "for your window. Pain."

Thought — well, thought I thought — how queer the world smacks its palms together for the sporting man, the brave one, the winner.

You don't have to be a genius, no Einstein, no Mozart, no Tolstoy even. Just a deadly clobberer of balls or a leg-jiggler or muscle-man and stap me! — the applause! My God, the roars of whacking approval, the enormous wide-spread glaze of idolatrous eyes. Slice atoms, reach moons, invent the jet — now who was that? But rub a piece of curved leather manfully across your jock strap (leaving an ambiguous stain), punt another piece two hundred yards, slice another down hissing fairways through miles of ignored dew and your name is the clue in the crossword, the proof of the after-shave, fridge, fag, stereo or dog food.

I thought of that.

I thought of that and I thought of that.

I've watched women on the telly crying in Israel and Syria and Palestine. I've watched them emptied out of their houses in Cambodia, Afghanistan, Soweto. I've watched them in the bread queues in Poland. And I've thought, "If only the men would go away."

So long ago now since I thought it out.

I come from a long line of men. This country tells me

132

this. Rams this home. Well, women enter into it, but peripherally.

(Lying here, staked out on my canvas fold-away by sun-slant in another town, watching the green bits of Judas tree through the open door, I am boss of this yard. This yard. This twelve by twelve. Table. Chair. A musing, maybe dying now, urgeless now, boss of one chair, one table, a mass of paints I haven't touched for months, two hundred badly stacked canvases and sketches and an atlas. I am becoming one who can be quiet in a room and stay there.

Perfectly content?

I say, tentatively as a baby mouthing, the word "life", and the word opens in and out like a squeeze-box as I notice the dry-rot working away at the window-frames but still clutching the glass between this and that, me and there.)

Do you remember your grandfather?

Nothing personal, but do you?

I remember mine only as a boisterous jogger through my father's stories dealt out at random into a scrubbed bedtime face. Poor old bloke, long gone now, all that vitality petered out, bunged into the silence but with me here still, me lying here, listening to my own silence padding up, and for me his shouting and racketing still go on.

"What was he really like?" I hug my knees under the fresh white sheets.

"Ah!" my father says. "I didn't know him much after I turned fourteen or so. Even before that. Except the odd time when he came to see me at school. Holidays he always seemed busy. Like with you, Gabby. You and Jam. I guess we don't know too much about each other."

"But what did he look like?"

I demand a god. This will be a little man, I dread, a

half-chap with a turned-in eye and too much hair or none.

"Not a bruiser. You wanted a bruiser, didn't you? A frontier gorilla. No, just an average looking man. About the body, that is. Something on the lean side. A traveller with a traveller's eyes."

(The atlas is for places I have never been.)

That's a phrase I suck along the edges of my tongue: a traveller with a traveller's eyes. When I look through the doorways, the windows of this stifler room and see through memory's telescope those hills which are suddenly become my dears, my darlings, I remember too those scab-knee years when I believed the world to have been minted purely for me.

Later, oh not so much later, I realized the liar globe offers itself fresh this way to every new generation, a pro whore with eternal youth, each new orb glistening with red green yellow and purple countries and untravelled spaces that the newcomer strains to like a wind.

My haunted old man tucks me in and forgets me behind some scrubby salt-bush of the mind, wanders down the track, hitting at bush-flies, lunging at shadows. Relaxed now, in my holiday shorts, lying there in high summer among my once and now dears of hills to see him move more ripely than I ever saw earlier in the way years have of sharpening the distant and dimming the present. Dad feller, lost convention-cluttered mum, Jam, Wafer, Moon. I see you now. I see. (The atlas really is for places I have never seen.)

As if to blot out the morning's waking, those horrible lantern slides of last night, I lie in the new day and think about my grandfather.

Granddad, Jam, me, ride saddle-slack into his first coast town.

This is the beginning of the journey.

Before this, who knows?

Not my father. All he ever learned was what his eyes and ears taught him about that over-confident bugger sitting his horse easy with his hat shoved back and teeth nibbling the chin-strap.

Why this obsession with origins? I confuse granddad's boyish laughter — I like that stereotype — with Jam's and mine. With Wafer's. Granddad didn't shave clean, and his hair flopped, flops, above the eyes, still boyish though that won't last long enough for dad to see.

The family's ships move like Circle Clippers along the trades.

Men need legends, my dad has told me. (Dad, this morning. Affectionately. Not father.) Need legends. Well, ours stops short or begins at a name plucked from a straight-laced British statesman three generations back and implanted in a pudgy opera singer of indifferent upper register. That's all my father tells me and all his father told him: a conception hurried over between one performance of Tosca and another in a hotel bedroom off Battery Point with the bouquets dying. To be sea-rocked hundreds of miles for more Toscas at the summer-cracked bottom of the continent and shot squalling into a mid-wife's arms in a dingy apartment in St Kilda. In four years time Tosca is to give charity concerts for the brave lads of Mafeking and sometimes, strapping her corsets around the stretch marks, she thinks of her squalling by-blow and posts off money, lockets on chains, concert programmes indelicately scented, silver spoons with back country town names on the handles and mock-soldier caps to an up-country farm in the Dandenongs.

From where? To what?

Oh yes, to what. To granddad. Ultimately, to my dad. Jam. Me.

I roll out of bed to Tottie's third impatient call from the

kitchen, wondering how to ignore father's craven apathy last night.

Perhaps he has told Tottie all about it over an early morning cup of tea — and when I see her she does have that abstracted look as if someone had shoved a dirty picture straight under her nose.

Wafer was gone only three days.

They stitched him up and sent him back in the same ambulance as Sergeant Cropper and Smiler.

As the New Year starts panting for us, Doss, Stobo, Emmie and I form a welcoming committee. Where are you Brim? Where are you Moon?

Timothy Rider has come pedalling out the lake-track on his bike and we discover that Moon is gone. He has driven his van down to Archie Wetters' old place, abandoning the bus-homestead, taking his blackness into the collapsing corners of the old girl's shack. I hate to think of him there.

Wafer, making satiric recovery, did paste a little notice to the glass the first day back, a celebration of Emmie's grim pun: pain. Doss hands round scones and coffee and we all gaze past the scarlet lettering at the bull-hide landscape and watch Colley come limping up the track, placing his feet carefully, doing fancy work with his walking-stick and pausing with artistic exhaustion on the verandah before dropping into a deck-chair.

All yesterday and last night rain had slashed at the landscape and the hillside runs with mud and small rivulets down into Wafer's head-bowed orchard. In this pause between bursts, great storm-heads keep rolling across and the heat shoves at the cloud to get through.

Over the lake, a kite hangs, lonely as the lot of us.

Colley is given to hand-rubbings of pleasure, the old

Smiler, stabilizing his unfailing belief in the good things of the world by our gathered presence. Supported by his smile.

And supported by a smile, shocking, he says, referring to what we all know. Shocking. The smile is even more open. More curly. It had worked wonders on nurses and a matron and even one of the junior doctors. After two weeks in hospital, his eye, cleared as he would have us believe, by suffering, is more bluely candid than ever. In the ambulance on the way home he had tried to register his horror at what had happened to Wafer but Cropper shut him up.

"And how are you?" He didn't want an answer. "My God," he said, "but that was a dreadful thing. And the whole town there. Why didn't your father . . . ?" Looking at me. I had no answer and Colley wanted none. "Destroys your faith in man," he said, "that sort of behaviour. Doesn't it?"

Wafer sat in an antibiotic haze.

"In father?" I asked.

"God no! Moon."

"What *is* your faith then, Tom?"

"You don't mean church of course." The old smile.

"No. I don't mean church. What do you believe in? Do you pin your faith on God or Emmie or books or money or jokes in the bar, in being one of the boys? What is it?"

Colley's smile slipped the merest fraction.

"Well," he said and gave a practised little pain wince, easing his leg, "God certainly comes into the picture sometimes, even though I think he's forgotten about me, maybe never heard of Allbut. Books? The last lasting escape. *My* bomb shelter for that matter. And other people. Yes. Other people. The wife when she was alive. Emmie." Saying Emmie's name gave him a wonderful confidence and he glanced slyly at Wafer whose now thinner face, the bony frame explicit, was uplifted to the rain-greys of the morning. "I guess we all believe in the basic decency of blokes. That might mean jokes in the bar, mightn't it? But all in all, the sense of what's right. What's fair."

Doss and Stobo took that as their cue to make their get-away. Just what we have to do right now, she said. Get back and open up. Floating between the good-byes came Emmie's voice repeating sadly "what's right, what's fair" and she got up and wandered after Doss and Fred, following them down the steps, across the soggy grass to their car.

"Have I said something!" Colley tried to look rueful but it wasn't in him. "I'd cross deserts on my knees for Emmie," he said, and we wanted to believe those words but they had the staleness, the glibness of over-use and Wafer picked up his cup and drained it off and asked Colley straight, "What are your politics?"

"Well, well!" the old Smiler cried. "What is this? Question time?"

Wafer looked away from him at a flock of corellas punctuating the trees at the lake edge, at Emmie watching them. As the kite planed down, the corellas screeched and in a minute the whole flock had rattled off across the water.

"I believe," Colley said gently wiping his curly mouth, "– Tim, why don't you join Emmie? – in the democratic rights of everyone." He looked up, candid, candid. No smile for this one. Behind us, Wafer's battery radio, wrinkled with static, was giving out the mid-morning news in bursts – *and fifteen hostages in the Cuban Embassy have so far been unable to negoti* – *say that no deputations on their behalf will be received* – The voice vanished and came back with a whoop – *the President* – and faded altogether.

Who, I ask myself, are the hostages? Those in Iran? Italy? Cuba? London? Allbut? Oh truly here in Allbut we are hostages as much as those fifty Yanks, six Londoners, twenty-three Cubans, the Italian Leader of the National Party, the three North Ireland coppers.

Could Wafer now move from this house and his few acres without the town falling on him? I sense the town wait. Moon waits across the tracks. And this man, this smiling Colley, is really here now to see the lie of the land.

"All men?"

"All men." Unblushingly Colley asks for more coffee. "Do you mind?"

"Help yourself."

"Of course," Colley added, sipping as if he were thinking deeply, "some yield their rights. Give them up, you might say, when they break the rules."

"You mean criminals?"

"Well, that's obvious of course. But not only them. Those who go against the wishes of the majority."

He looked down cunningly.

"Give me a case then," Wafer suggested suicidally. "A case in point."

I felt I should go away, follow Emmie, follow Timothy. It was frightful watching old Smiler set his blatant traps.

"But there are thousands of those. You know it. We all know it."

"What about those hostages on the news just now? What about them? Does a hostage forfeit all rights?"

Colley looked over at Wafer with his lower lip stuck to the rim of a thoughtful cup, his eyebrows pressed into a frown over the frank blue.

"If," he said, "if they *were* working against their host country, and there were certain indications that they might have been, then perhaps that country has a point, don't you think? After all, they're guests as it were."

"Like me?"

"I don't follow," Colley said quickly, pretending badly.

Each bone of Wafer's face appeared to pose a question that demanded answers. His knobby angles made me as well as Colley uncomfortable, Colley with his gammy leg and the bugger of a chair he couldn't fit himself to.

It was guilt with me.

"I'm the newcomer here," Wafer admitted. "But then so are you. The new boy. Oh there's a pattern I well remember. The bullies. The clique you couldn't break into no matter how you tried. A classic pattern. I'm a hostage too."

"Oh God, old man, what makes you think that? Don't take it like that. It's not like that at all."

"I don't know what else it's like."

"Come on, old chap, you're not an embassy!" Colley laughed vigorously at his joke trying to pin me in with his eye.

"In a way," Wafer said.

"In a way what?"

"An embassy. This is an embassy. This. All this. It's my bit of territory in an alien stink-hole" — he was surprised to hear himself call Eden that! — "and I have diplomatic immunity."

Colley used his handkerchief again. "No. No. I don't think you quite have that. Not once you've shared part of this little town. This little democracy." And the old bastard grinned.

"Democracy!" Wafer spat the word.

"Made use of it," Colley went on ignoring Wafer's interruption. "I feel the same about it myself, that I owe, since I've — well, touched its edges. Even its edges. You do know."

"Oh but I don't."

Colley pulled a face.

"Well, take Emmie," he said flatly, eyes on Wafer's, open and waiting, waiting to receive.

Wafer's hands jerked into his thighs where the ache there must have attacked him like a false witness.

The kite above the lake had been joined by another and farther out now they practised their deadly geometry in sheer emptiness.

The three of us avoided looking at Emmie who was walking back across the paddock with young Rider in new spatterings of rain.

Then Colley was mumbling.

"Emmie's told me."

"Emmie's told you what?"

"Don't force me, old man. I'm trying to keep it friendly."

"Told you what?"

"Well, she was in bed with you, wasn't she?"

"She told you that?"

"It's true, isn't it?"

"The accidents may be true. The substance is false."

"Oh don't blind me with philosophy, old chap," Colley protested. "Don't do that. Mind you, I had to prise it out of her. Cropper tipped me off. Didn't like to mention it while you were in hospital there with that rotten injury. The way she told it —"

He stopped and chewed on a match before he lit his cigarette. "Gabby, do you mind?" (Playing courtly gentlemen!)

"Oh don't let's be nice," Wafer said. "There'll be Emmie in a moment and young Rider too. Now. What way?"

"Look," Colley protested, inhaling deeply, shooting protective smoke screens all round him, the smile gone, "Look, no matter how it *was*, it looks bad. Bloody bad. You can see that, can't you? Not that I think for a minute that you — that Em —. It's not good for the kid and it's not good for you. Especially for you. If I wanted — and I'm not like that at all, really — but if I wanted, I could make trouble. After all, she's under age."

Wafer rose abruptly, grimacing past me, taking more than his weight on his wounded groin, and went in from the verandah. Through the window of his tiny living-room, the lost dog that was Colley's face followed him with wagging inquiry.

"There's no arguing with you, is there?" Wafer said.

His voice sharpened with pain and anger floating out across the verandah, across the last stretch of grass to Emmie and young Rider who were running from the rain. Even the kites could pick up the scraps. "No reasoning with you. None. It's not the truth of the matter, just the appearances."

Colley smiled helplessly. He had really been terribly straightforward about it.

"That's all, old man."

Wafer limped back to the verandah. He didn't seem to notice the rest of us, his eyes stabbing into Colley's.

"Tell me what you want."

Colley didn't hesitate. "It's not up to me. Not just me. It's the rest of them. The town." He gazed up at Wafer with his honest sky-blue eyes. "Moon told you what we wanted. You said you would, remember?"

"And if I don't?"

Colley told him.

They gave him a few days' grace, time for the wound to heal.

After all, the new and smiling year was only five days old. The Christ Child was forgotten.

On his second night back from hospital Wafer began stacking his possessions, removing his jocular walled aphorisms, hesitating over the last on his window and leaving it here. He left it along with the unfinished St Francis. He closed the trap-door on his shelter. Had he really been serious about that? And after he had finished the tedious and painful packing of the van, he made himself a last coffee on the primus, sitting in the ten o'clock dark, listening to the rain stride across his roof.

There was still a light showing in Colley's shack and briefly he thought about Emmie in her bed, narrow, wretched thoughts.

One thing he couldn't leave. A year ago in Mainchance's pioneers' museum he had bought a small off-set pocket history of Allbut. Among the settler-dressed dummies, dusty and broken cradles, miners' lamps, pickaxes, taipans in bottles, tin-ware, rock samples and gemstones, he had found half a dozen of the booklets lying dusty on a piano hauled in from the coast for the wing-dings, the church society revels, whacked by thumpers till the sound-board had cracked in the dry winters and the Wet had grown a loving moss across the felts.

The poorly written tenderly felt pages lay before him under lamp-light and now, sipping his last coffee this last night, he shuffled the pages, reading the names of the mines and claims as if they were talismanic: The Hurricane, The Brass jar, The Wowser, The Earth Turned Over. Those names, along with the men who worked them, in the hopeful sadness of their present, blinked, glow-worm tiny from the page: Wattie Swan, Manny Totten, Arch Kerridge, Moses Wade (who were you, Moses Wade?) and Pico Santarelli. Pico? Where are you now, Pico? Does anyone now remember the sweating gold sheen of your seven horse dray, the tin battery at Go-ahead, the time Chappie Gordon was rolled down the winze? The crumbled pubs? The Miners' Arms Dance Hall? Tommy Knee and Ah Tong with pack horses traipsing fruit and vegetables, the teamsters dragging groceries from the coast, the fire at the Wombat's Pleasure? Gracie Tilburn up to stay with a greying aunt at Allbut and singing dabs from Our Miss Gibbs, The Gipsy Baron, The Chocolate Soldier?

Wafer flicked back to the front of the stapled pages.

His coffee had grown cold for eighty or ninety years but the conversational and rambling prose re-vitalized those long-gone. He wanted to cry. His lost refuge confronts him with a wall of bush timbers and a tacked up poster of the ruins at Chichen Itza he had left for irony's sake. He is there, eighty years away, in the lost Allbut. He reads down the page and Pico Santarelli starts walking his dray over to Moses Wade who stands, legs apart, in his moleskins and snake-boots outside Skipper Noonan's Emporium that no longer exists the moment he looks up.

Oh the pointlessness of the struggle simply to be. Like Moses Wade, Wattie Swan, Arch Kerridge, Chichen Itza and the Indians had crop trouble, bouts of constipation in Coba, Ichpatun, Chunyaxche.

Restless he rose and walked the small length of the verandah for the last time. He was wired in with rain and could see the lake like a blank medal.

Where are the swans on the dam?

Where are the beautiful white birds that came as a gift to the first settlers in the town, the mini-empire that fostered Manny Totten, Wattie Swan, Moses Wade and Pico Santarelli?

(I have read Wafer's little history. I have my own copy. And who will write about Wafer? No one except me. And do I matter?

See him. I paint him in the shaking circle of kerosene light which on those yellowing pages is the only communion bread. But perhaps across the slope of the lake's hip Colley and his daughter sit below other pools of light like communion breads and think about him.

Then he turns back into his unpeopled room, his

honourableness stuck like a judgmental lump in the throat.

Nothing left now but the poster, a few records he could no longer bear to play, some books and a dirty coffeecup not quite empty, the lamp and this yellow circle.

The yellow circle and his lean shadow trying to hide in the wall behind.)

He fumbled in his shirt pocket for his note book and a pencil stub. Both of them wanted to write Emmie a poem, even more than he, as the pencil lay on the diary page, waiting for him to begin.

Dear Emmie, he wrote, I wanted to leave you some kind of lyric but I haven't your strength or your ability. But if I write two simple sentences you will understand them.
There is a pool of light on my table, a golden circle.
I am turning it out.

He didn't get far.

They let him think himself safely away for the rest of the night, ruptured as it was by the groaning guts of his van as he skidded out along the dirt road from the lake into town.

The world was full of drizzle, pain in his groin and a gumminess of air through which the monument displayed briefly in his headlights its own vermilion scar. The town let him go. The pub. The police station. The two stores. The shire office. The empty school. The School of Arts sleeping with its dried up arteries of yellow red and white. He drove by the dreaming windows, past the rusted heaps ditched in storm channels that were now awash with water; past the galvanized humpies of the blacks' camp; past the sign that said Allbut.

If he avoided Mainchance and took the northeast road it was four hundred kilometers of corduroy before he came to the next town on the mainline training east. But he couldn't expect to make it before morning with the range shelves between him and it, complicated with gasps of turns and sudden sheer threats. As he drove, the world thickened with trees and fear-struck animals trapped in carlight, rain belching silver over the whole worldscape and his wipers unable to cope. The road was hardly used now except for station owners getting out to the coast and the blue kombi vans of new life-stylers the map had filled up with. His mind and the world were gullies and scarps.

Not to think.

The motor lugged midnight into two into four at a bare twenty-five chug up the gravel road of the spine, down the eastern slope into five o'clock and the bitumen by six with the rain gloomily steady as he took the last straight fifty kilometers into the first township.

He was sagging at the wheel, half sleeping but aware of the petrol gauge quivering down on the red. He had used up the spare can of petrol he carried over an hour ago. Scrub was becoming paddocks, the ruined fences of old huts asleep in the mist that hung round them like mosquito netting; was becoming the scarlet cries of neglected flame trees run to seed. By the time he reached the outskirts of the township, limp sunlight was trying to cut through the clouds that kept rolling steadily across, the blacktop spun like glass and the first houses began. Slow breakfast signals rose above their roofs.

It was a small town.

Another one, he thought. One of those. But it had a cafe and a garage at the end of the main street.

He drove past the stores, the little cluster of houses lumped together for safety, past the cafe and parked outside the petrol station.

There was still a capful of coffee left in his thermos and almost too exhausted to think he sat there, drinking slowly, blowing the weak steam across the cup lip and clouding the windscreen. Tell yourself, he kept telling himself he told me, there's the whole map to course. The atlas is for places he has never seen. He could drive that old crate anyplace, anyplace at all, he assured himself bitterly, as long as there's a lake, hill arms and a young girl as part of it.

"I have no time at all, Lionel," his Uncle Bedwetter *in loco parentis* was saying in the driver's window, bristling and bullish to his fifteen year old pimples, "for this dreamy — what shall I say? — otherness. You hardly seem to know whether you're coming or going these days. *Do* you know? Buggering about. Driving your mother and me crazy. I mean what *is* this?" He was waving a school report straight into Wafer's sleepless face. "There's a little too much of your mad Aunt Clancy in you, lad. Of course you've got to bloody play football. Of course you've got to join cadets. Christ, what's wrong with you? You really didn't say this to old Hunnicutt, did you?"

"What does he say I said?"

"That's you all over, isn't it? Temporize. Temporize." His uncle glared at him before he read the vile words out. "He says you said," — looking up, hardly believing this — "he says that you said male group activities of this violent nature were a sop to homosexual proclivities and you preferred — you *preferred!* — not to be so co-erecd. My God! I don't, I simply don't believe it. A nephew of mine! What would your father . . . "

Sitting there remembering.

Never one for co-ercion, for the group activity, the fun in the locker room, the drinks with the boys, the bar dirt, national mateship. Not even conscious of tabulations of time, of years. It had driven Ruth mad, that vagueness, after she had stopped loving him for it. Never one of those people who could say with party-line dogmatism it was in the second half and Troggers dropped the ball just as he was taking a pass from Fatcherley or Brisbane, dear, it was Brisbane right on the Ides of March don't you remember no I don't remember and I don't remember that little tennis wonder sending a lob to the serve-line and following up with a sliced smash to the far court or that it was sixty-eight just after

Christmas that you had the kitchen re-vamped or the exact date they murdered the president, anyway which president, wound up world war two, stopped the draft. As if — as if they were the ultimate generation.

The folly of that thinking, yet once he too had felt that seed, that most dangerous seed, he decided, sprouting within himself: that badging error of youth that made one believe in one's primacy — or ultimacy.

Two thousand million years from protozoa to this, the I of me, muscle-trim for a few decades and thinking snappy, the ultimate aim of all that wriggling pond life, me. Me and my contemporaries. The world, ignoring the ripe brains-trust of early philosophers, has worked its way towards me, us, now: an anarchic world of money-grabbing, fast food bars, asylum advertising that refuses to accept its repeated mediocrity.

And now, how quickly that flare of personal importance dies down.

There was already another be-fooled generation breathing on his neck — the Emmies, the Timothys, thinking precisely the same thing about itself, miscalculating its importance, making the same moral misjudgements as he now stuck with years and wilting on the edge of discovery.

His real discovery came with sun-up.

His watch showed seven-thirty.

He had dozed a bit and was woken by a grunting utility rumbling down the street from west to east. At ten to eight, again nudging him from uneasy half-asleep, the cafe door unlocked protestingly and a few minutes after that a boiler rooster with a comb of ginger hair rolled out of the house behind the petrol pump, hawked, spat, stared at Wafer's van and went back inside.

Wafer creaked out of the van and went after him.

He knocked for quite a while on the hall beside the open front door to a smell of bacon and burnt bread, learning the hallway lino pattern by heart. There were off-stage voices and crashings and finally a woman with her hair in plaits over a man's dressing-gown came and inspected him through the screen door.

After he had stuffed apologies through the mesh he requested petrol.

"We're not open yet," the woman said. She had nervous brown eyes and a small twitch.

"When do you open?"

"My husband deals with that side of it."

She seemed to be inspecting him with too much interest. Some front hair fell down.

"Well, could I see him?"

Her bare feet flopped away down the hall and there was the smack of a utensil being slammed. Wafer, all ear, heard a grunt and then a laugh.

The next moment the man's bulk was shouldering the walls back each side of the passageway as if he were the house itself sauntering towards Wafer. The rain had started again, heavily.

Behind the screen the red haired bloke loomed over Wafer who observed traces of grin and bacon fat about his mouth.

"What's your problem, mate?"

"My tank's empty. Your wife said you weren't open yet but I do want to get on. Can you fill her up?"

The rooster leant one hairy arm on the door jamb and regarded Wafer as if the matter bored him. With his other hand he wiped away some grease and mirth.

"Got none, mate."

"What do you mean?"

"What I said. No petrol. The tanker isn't due through here till Thursday. It's Monday now and that means you got a three day wait. More, maybe, with the holidays just over. Anyway, I only have enough for the locals. You aren't a local, are you?"

150

"Look," Wafer argued, "it's a hundred miles to the next town. My tank's empty. You can't do this. Legally you can't do this."

The man's eyes grew small. A whole new set of lines appeared across his forehead.

"Don't tell me, mate, what I can or can't do. I said no petrol and I mean no petrol."

At the back of the house a phone began to cluck.

"You get that, love?" the man asked without turning.

He moved one hand down the side of the door until he found the knob and still looking at Wafer started to close the door.

"What you really mean," Wafer began to cry angrily through the narrowing space, "is you've got no petrol for me."

"That's about it, mate," the man said.

The door clicked shut.

Christ, thought Wafer, oh God oh mateship oh generous long lean fellers of the bush myth the helping hand you only got to shout can't do enough for me mates. Shit, he said aloud, and began to hammer on the wall's bland surface uselessly, gave up, and flung his limp down the path to the van.

He drove the fifty yards or so back up the main street to the railway station, a shed not much bigger than an outhouse. If, he was reasoning, if I lock the van and simply leave it, later a trucking company can pick it up and bring it down to the coast. Or not bring it. Did he care, anyway? Why not let it die here along with all the other dead cars that litter the west.

There was a kid attendant doing things with a hard broom in the tiny waiting-room. The words sieved through freckles.

"There's a rail-motor this arv," he said. He kept sweeping listlessly then leaned. "Three ten. But it's going out to Mainchance. The coast mail doesn't come through till Thursday."

"With the petrol tanker?"

"Eh?" the kid said.

"Ah forget it!"

"There's a goods train, eh. She goes through round about six. You can get a ticket on that if you like."

Wafer inspected the harmless unrazored face.

"All right," he said. "Give me a single."

"Sorry, mister. The ticket office don't open till just on train time. Get you one then, eh."

Wafer shrugged. The nightmare was becoming farce.

He went back to the van, pulling out his shoulder bag, locked up and walked back to the cafe.

The fly hazard. The three tables, all wobblers. The disappointed waitress. The lumped up sugar. The dripping tea pot.

"We've come a long way since that pond," he told himself as he cut into the underdone and leaking eggs.

It was eight-fifteen.

I am the omniscient narrator. I am a weaver of knowns and almost knowns. I translate. I paraphrase. It's all legal in a *confessio amantis*.

Wafer dreamt he was inside a giant translucent stone running with blue and citrine fire, faceted so that impossibly, internally, images of himself held in glass moved as he moved, clawed walls as he clawed, smiled, wept and punched until knuckles echoed their bruising at the invisible barriers in multiple reduplication.

Through streaks of indigo and lemon he caught part glimpses of Emmie and her father dancing slowly and gravely in time to Moon who, perched on a hill of sapphire, strummed a guitar in the sad progressions of a saraband. Someone was singing, high-pitched and fearful, a cante jondo.

The monochrome sculpture of the music moved from no sense to sense and Wafer heard as he felt he had heard once before the words:

Cerco tiene la luna

mi amor ha muerto.

The moon is fenced in, the voice kept singing. My love has died.

Moon's lips moved but the sound came from Wafer himself as he writhed in his crystalline chamber. Yellow flooded his eyes to pressed lemons and in the blink-space he saw Emmie and her father dancing away, measured, deliberate, into a curtain of dusty grey scrub that opened and closed like stage draperies.

"Emmie!" he shouted noiselessly through blinding lemon. "Emmie!"

The rock smacked the sound back into his bursting ears and the blood throb in them and in his heart and the voice of the singer mated with the yellow light coasting his transparent lids.

He was being nudged awake with a bluntly-intentioned boot.

"Wakey wakey!"

Wafer was lying on the rock-hard seat of the station waiting-room.

The rain had gone and the early afternoon sun was branding his face so that he could hardly open his eyes for the scald of it. He shaded them with one hand and squinted into the faces looking down on him through the gone tide of sleep. Groggily Councillor Brim's and Sergeant Cropper's features swam into shape.

This can't be, he thought. Though he had expected it all along.

Cannot be.

(You gaze at ocean or river or bay and there is no pic-

153

ture, only a vast swinging green to fill the whole canvas. "Now put a tree there," my first art teacher had suggested ever so nicely. "And then you have water through branches." Leaves are a kind of word. You have a picture. This Monday of Wafer's. Blank, really, with only a twelve hour road scrawled roughly across its twelve hour map. Bung these two fellers on the road behind him; fill them up with crazy logic and suddenly the map becomes a problem in journeying. He told me that once during boy-manoeuvres with boy-cadets, forced into the group at last, he had become so bored during parade he had stalked off, saying to the school sergeant, "Shoot me.")

So he said jauntily now:

"You're coming too?"

Their raised eyebrows lowered briefly as he muzzily rubbed his eyeballs clear with bunched knuckles and longed for a pee.

"Having a little kip?"

Sergeant Cropper's playfulness held threat, his grin a hoon compound of tombstone white and gold fillings.

Wafer swung his legs to the ground, sat up and looked from one to the other while Councillor Brim dropped his eyes.

"I'm waiting for the train."

"You can't be doing that," Sergeant Cropper corrected gently. "You're coming back with us."

Wafer's stomach lurched. He wanted to laugh but nervously.

"Coming back with you, for God's sake. Why would I be doing that?"

"You've had a little taste," Cropper said. "There's not much else you can do, is there Jim?" Councillor Brim gave a mandarin nod. "You really shouldn't have pulled out like that, not with unfinished business. Not after what you said you'd do. Sneaked out, really. It gives a bad impression."

"Oh fuck off!" Wafer said.

Cropper's big paw smacked him lightly on the cheek.

Agog in the waiting-room doorway, the porter stood open-mouthed his freckles standing out with interest.

"Language!" Cropper warned. "Language, mate. I could take you in for using obscene language in a public place."

"I'm catching the train," Wafer insisted.

"Listen," Cropper said. "Do I have to spell it out? You're coming back with me. There's a couple of things that need to be talked over. Normally I'd be glad to see the back of you, mate, but there's that little matter of the kid for a start. Either you come nicely or we throw the book at you."

"You'd better come, Wafer," Councillor Brim urged a little shamefacedly. He knew more about the humiliations of daily living than Cropper.

Wafer looked at him and then back at Cropper. "The little matter of the kid, you said. You mean Emmeline Colley. There was nothing there. Nothing. Nothing you could lay a charge about. Simply – nothing."

"You don't seem to understand," Cropper explained patiently. "It doesn't matter there was nothing. There might have been nothing and then again there mightn't. To be frank, mate, I believe you. But it's the suggestion of it. The smell. It only has to be suggested on a complaint from the father and it doesn't matter a stuff whether there was or there wasn't. You're still for a charge, up for a carno. And after you've fought your way out of that one, you still stink. You stink and the kid stinks. There's a very nasty smell." He turned to the gawper and said kindly, "Piss off, sonny."

Wafer was beaten out. Breakers of incapacity kept washing through a drumming rain which had started

155

again with the suddenness of the wet. It was hopeless. This town like a patch of scrub itch. The clangour on the tin roof. His bag at his feet.

"I have here," Cropper was saying, "a formal complaint from Mr Colley" (of the smile, the curls, the candid blue eye). "Now it's simply up to you. You come along nicely with us and do that other little thing we asked about and I tear this up. We forget about it. And when you've done that, someone will run you back here. You'll find your tank filled, maybe even a bit of air in your tyres, and off you go, free as a breeze."

"You're the one that stinks," Wafer said without emphasis.

"Careful. That tank could stay empty a long time, matey. Think about it. You don't want me to make a fuss, do you?"

A ute splashed in through the railway gates and nosed to a stop beside some rolling-stock. The driver leaned out his cab window and raised one arm in a careless way to Cropper who gave a half-wave back.

"You know everyone," Wafer commented with pique, remembering the garage owner, the phone call.

"It's my business. I know them all. Well, what's it to be?"

The dream was almost erased now but there was a sudden flicker of blue-green glimpsed through partings in the dusty scrub as Emmie danced gravely alone, her almost adult face turning once to look at him. Once. The curtains of scrubs closed.

"Don't make a mistake now," Cropper advised leaning heavily towards Wafer. "Don't make a wrong decision, mate, because we'll make you come anyway."

That's how it happened. That's how they got him back for the last act.

But there was more.

While Wafer was being hauled through the tyrant hills, Moon returned to the lake that morning after Emmie had driven Smiler into town for stores, for conspiracy, for who knows what.

(I am painting Smiler and each over-white tooth is a cameo setting for each of our ruined faces. Interesting, this, our blackest natures on a background of finest ivory.)

He did the simple thing, Moon. He set a charge in Wafer's shelter and blew the lot sky-high. The whump of it reached town, reaching me mooning over morning coffee on the verandah. "What's that?" Jam asked curiously who had come in for a quick coffee. "Someone's life gone up," I said without looking at him. I remember this clearly. "You do talk a lot of crap, sis," he said, wolfing a sandwich and gulping his coffee.

And after that, Moon flung kerosene around as if preparing for an auto da fé and inspired by the blaze moved his darkness down to Colley's shack and burnt that too. The wild flowers of crackling light must have run like creepers up and over the walls, down through the timber rooms until their insane blossoming collapsed in ashes.

It must have been Moon.

It was.

I saw him.

After Jam had left for the yards I got out my runabout and drove to the lake. It took only ten minutes. What made me park my car at the turn-off, stay it cautiously in a side track under a scrub shield? Smoke warned me, but more than that, some primitive conviction of something wrong. I walked in, cutting over the spur and leaving the track.

Below me, just below, Wafer's house was fully ablaze.

I won't say I helped Moon do it. But I watched him.

And it was then.

I saw Moon coming out of the double-decker he'd used for his pad carrying two jerry-cans, striding bare-headed and concentrated across the long slope to Colley's. And I watched, oh I watched all right, as he paused on the little verandah, unscrewed one of the cans and started splashing stuff around. For a minute I lost sight of him when he went inside and yes, I knew what he was doing. Even before his second bonfire I knew, and did nothing. I did nothing as the roof fell in like a brilliant autumn. I did nothing.

I watched him go. I heard him start his van and I heard the sound die away along the lake road. Yet even then I couldn't bear to go down and look at what he and I had achieved.

I waited until a fresh rain-burst drove me. The flames were puttering out now and smoke was thickening up the whole canvas.

Wafer's house was gone, bits of his things scattered down the track below as if a wind had torn them out. Those bits and pieces. I kept hearing him say that the contents or heart of a house were a substitution of knowledge for the ignorance most people have about their internal organs.

This body was eviscerated.

I gape at this emptiness hearing his voice, calm, explanatory, telling me, too, how this place of his had been an attempt to cut through the anonymous suburb sprawl where houses repeated their external parts in the manner of nightmare. How, he had marvelled, did anyone find a way back to the right hutch? He'd marvelled until the time came when he lived in a similar hutch so twinned with its neighbours he realized he carried around with him like conscience, like liver and lights, the more intimate anatomy of its four small rooms – the disposition of books, of stains, of a red bowl on a sink, an unmade bed, the exploding gas heater.

All down the track on the soaking grass were fragments of his chairs, his table, his camp stretcher. There were record shards and some pages of exercise book blown onto the rock-crops.

I walked down slowly, close to tears, between the charred timbers of what was once a verandah and my heart stuffed up as I squatted amongst the still warm ashes where records had melted and welded into wavy hat-brims. I turned the smouldering pile over with a small stick. Haydn's Surprise Symphony half-said the label, under the lost memory of the jokey placards and the poster of the ruins at Chichen Itza.

I stood up, slowly, not caring about the rain now, letting it belt my hair flat to my head, letting it cry harder than I ever could, and looked down at the smoking mess of Colley's house, down past the sharp snow of asbestos segments scattered everywhere between the rocks, and slowly, deliberately drowning in sky-grief, I began to walk the track for the last time, sensing there was nothing left for me here.

Not quite nothing.

Wafer's little note-book lay sodden in the grass a few feet away from the remains of his stretcher. Just the smallest memento, I told myself, blown out by the blast. The very smallest.

So I picked it up from where it lay open on the grass, turning the wet pages carefully, the wet pages of reminders, grocery lists and idiot notations, until I came to the last thing he had written.

I found my heart racing as if it were about to take a terrible jump.

The smoke still oozed up and away from Smiler's shack. The lake remained expressionless.

159

Standing there, I read his last message to Emmie watching the ink run as I read.

That is all. I read it.

I understand images in my slap-dash amateur fashion. And it was the explicitness of those words that enraged and despaired me.

I read them over and over.

I knew the note by heart and it rang like a love letter of the most delicate intensity light years away from Torben, Willi, Sam, Jackson.

I hated it. I tore it up.

Then I went back to my car and sat there, howling like a dog, while the rain sobbed outside the glass and the smoke died away and I kept being aware of my greatest failure of all: the failure to inspire the gentleness of love. You always get out of things what you put into them, father had said, but always my emotional change seemed smaller than the amount I had spent: the first horse I gave three months' grooming and training threw me at the local show; the first boy I hero-worshipped said "But you're some kind of nutter!"; when I hung my first art school efforts in the bar of the Wowser, there was total silence and Mrs Brim said to my mother, "She always was a strange girl."

I don't know how long I sat inspecting the fever-rash of personal failure but the rain eased along with my tears and through the watery sun I had a vision of Moon, head springing horns and bounding light-footed to create two terrible bursts of summer.

The worse half of me was glad.

As I drove back to town through mid-day I knew that if anyone had said "Own up the person who did that", I should have cried Oh it was me me me it was me.

Wafer was dumped smack into the middle of an assembly of town elders.

Where? I ask Doss Campion that next morning.

She answered with a pithy comment on the nature of men, questioned the sanity of the town, nodded in a cautionary way at the presence of Emmeline who had been left by Smiler (they were stopping at the pub in their homeless state) and nodded in the general direction of the School of Arts. Smiler's racking sobs had taken him damwards.

I could hardly face Emmie, her doubtful smile cutting into my knowledge. The town is ready to blame anyone for the fire — passing tramps, a secretly returned circus hand, a travelling rep — anyone but a townsman. The town has forgotten Christmas, forgotten the New Year with its inane promise of renewal and I have forgotten my sudden love affair with the town.

"They've gone to the School of Arts," Emmie said bleakly, "before it falls down." I shouldn't have laughed but I did and she looked at me soberly and added, "And they won't want any women there."

Oh Emmeline Colley how well you understand that strutting male self-importance at thirteen, are you? You'll be safe in this world, for I never learnt the way you have.

But I learnt when I walked through the musty doors of the old building, for father and Jam came from the table where they were seated with Wafer and asked me to leave. Father, give him credit, looked uncomfortable, and I stared over his shoulder to where Wafer sat like a convict between Cropper and Brim, his tired face white and grimy.

Even now. Even now.

I obliged father yet after I had walked away a few yards the arrogance of his dismissal hit me — women are never quite adults — so I went round the back of the hall and found my way quietly to the change-room just off-stage in which the remains of the Allbut library mouldered in wasps' nests and dirt. Through a small window I could see into the hall where, enter Stobo and Moon, hippofooted under cartons.

Moon looked like a man without a memory.

My inner self advised against staying. I stayed.

I wanted to see if father and Jam were traitors like me. There's nothing like the comfort of knowing it runs in the family.

Cropper was rapping for silence, not that there was much need for the gesture but you could tell he thought it the proper, the formal thing to do. The others seemed careful not to look at Wafer or each other and there was not much talk for they weren't all bastards, those table-elders, mainly simple fellows, fed to the teeth with never having made it, pricked by dreams that meant escape into power, the heaven of money. There was some excuse — we're all greedy — but not for father, not for Jam, least of all for me. Cropper's bully-brain was now thinking for all of them.

Wafer appeared to have grown thin in his clothes.

There were a lot of words from the sergeant.

I suppose had I stalked in to that male chapel and reported what I had seen at the lake, I could have

162

changed the course of things. But I was full of jealous spite as well as the concern that went on and on.

"Looks like we're all set," Sergeant Cropper was saying heavily, cocking half a bull eye at the beer. "Wafer's showing us the place, doing the right thing by the town and we have Councillor Brim without whose help etcetera to thank. How's about a small hand for Councillor Brim."

They gave a small hand, even father who always acted in reflex.

It was almost absurd, like a rotary meeting.

"And now, just as a kind of good luck toast to our little exploring party, Fred's been nice enough to bring along some grog. Thanks, Fred, for all of us." His formal good cheer manner was falling like weights on Wafer. "Not that you're a crim," Cropper had explained when the police van had pulled up the evening before outside the Allbut Station. "Well, not yet. But you'll have to kip down in the lock-up."

Wafer had said he preferred to sleep at the pub.

"Oh I don't think so." Cropper had given a wink. "Doss has enough on her plate. And she's rather partial to you. I wouldn't want any interference at this stage. Bit of a Crusader, the old Doss. Always looking for lame dogs. Anyway, you'll have the cell to yourself. It hasn't seen a boong for a week."

The men were gulping their beer fast; one time they could have done without it, filled with an anxiety to be on the road. Stobo spilled an opened can down Wafer's front while Wafer was harried with questions about distances, directions that he fielded as if he meant to get the whole mad business over with. He sat there, a lonely birthday boy, until one carton emptied, not touching his beer but staring out the doors. From where I nosed against the streaked glass I could hang to the arc of his eye as if it were my own.

163

The minutes trudged.

Then Stobo began clearing things away and Cropper was whacking his ham fist on the table again and in the silence that followed Wafer's eye met Moon's and there seemed to be a strange mating as if they were discovering halves of some frightful whole.

"Okay, now," Cropper said. He stood taller than the rest, heavier, redder. Flecks of beer scum hung along his lower lip. "It's time we got started. Jim and me'll take Wafer along with us and you other blokes can sort yourselves out. Shove the rest of the beer in one of the vans. It's going to be a long hot day."

The men piled outside under the pepper trees.

I stood there, watching them go, in that back porch that smelt of withered paper and cardboard and dust, wondering, even then, if I should button-hole Cropper or father before the vans began to move away and accuse Moon. And every time I had half-convinced myself into striding, frank and sunny like old Colley, down those steps, and hurling my news, the small bomb of my witnessing, Wafer's last words to Emmie spread watery and large across my mind denying me a state of grace. "I am turning it out." I say the words, listening treacherously to the slamming of car doors and the splutter over of the first motor. "I am turning it out." The words become mine, then, mine, and I wobble outside into the steam after rain to find father talking with Jam.

"Aren't you going then?" I ask.

Father's eyes widened. "You still here? I thought you'd gone." He's hating the whole business, I can see.

I asked again.

"No." He gave his long-suffering look. "For God's sake, no."

"Why were you here, then, with that sick Star Chamber? Oh don't answer. Look. I'm going with Jam."

"I can't stop you," the old man said. "But Jam won't

164

want you. They'll none of them want you. Especially Wafer."

I found his hand on my shoulder and for a moment he looked so kind, so worried about me, about all of it, tears started to roll out of my eyes before I could turn away.

"If you only knew," I said. "If you only knew."

Then I started to run after Jam's truck which was just backing to turn and Moon who was sitting behind him said, I heard him say, "What's your bloody sister doing? We're not taking her," but Stobo leaned over the tail-board shouting to Jam to slow down and called, "Jump up, Gabby. There's room here."

Before Moon could get another word out of his scowling face I was hauled over the back-board and sprawling on a couple of hessian bags in a clutter of picks and gads.

Stobo looked at me with a whimsical grin. I like Fred.

"God, girl," he said. "It's like the rush." And laughed.

Wafer, wedged in the front of Cropper's four-wheel drive was thinking muzzily "What now? What do I tell them? Where do we go?"

He couldn't remember except in the cloudiest way where he'd camped that night he'd found the stone, his soured lump of luck. The direction he'd been taking the night before his discovered Eden held fragmented snapshots of granite hills and once a ghost cemetery of three graves with rubber-vines strangling the poinciana trees. This landscape was measureless, had no horizons. And what was the point? All they wanted was for him to find something, an eldorado of the mind much like his own that occupied Brim's and Cropper's concentrated eyes, their stretched out throats, as much as a royal flush on poker nights. In fifty years, thirty, probably twenty, it wouldn't matter to any of them. Couldn't they see that?

Crossing the landscape he had driven through a score of abandoned mining towns, grieving places of fallen roofs, the stump foundations of shanties whose tin walls lay drowned in nettles, skeleton sheds picked clean by scroungers, boarded-up pit-heads and rusting pieces of tramline, boiler and stamper. At the end of grass-shrouded tracks the flame of poinsettia still burning where someone seventy years gone had made a garden under lemon and tamarind trees gone scrubby; and when he had pulled in to poke about the unused mining tracks, the remnants of pub and shack, the wind whistled the marrow out of his bones. How could all that hugger-mugger living be nothing now?

As this now was to be nothing.

Moving from nothing to nothing as far as the world counts — saints, criminals, Long Island millionaires, public service stenographers, doormen, never-to-be-heard-of primitives in remote floating islands, factory workers, headline makers, Bombay cripples, Colombian hillsmen, 42nd street pimps, tarts, junkies — all briefly moving, flashing a small light, signalling for help.

And life gave barely enough time for the nine flashes — three short, three long, three short.

If he closed his eyes, he thought, squinting against the after-rain sun-glare, he could obliterate the car, his oaf captors and the dust smudge behind that meant Stobo and Moon and whatever stinking mat-folders they'd rung in.

Cropper's elbow caught him sharply in the ribs.

"Eyes open, matey. You're the one taking us for God's sake."

"Miles off yet," Wafer replied. "Miles. We haven't reached the coast turn-off."

"How many miles? How many past the turn-off?"

Think of a number. Any number. "Thirty," he said. To save himself he added, "Forty perhaps." He could remember a network of dying roads. "Take the next eastern fork after you reach the turn-off and run north for a bit. Now, can I just have a bit of shut-eye."

"No shut-eye," Cropper said. "We might miss the turn. There's a mass of side-tracks up that way but I don't know of any eastern fork off that road in the first fifty miles."

Wafer mumbled that he might have misjudged.

"You just keep watching. This isn't the time for little memory lapses. There's at least half a dozen roads heading off God knows where; old snigging trails, miners' tracks and even cattle pads that look like the real thing."

Wafer lied stubbornly. "The first you come to. The first. I said that."

Cropper seemed amused.

"You did. So you did. Bear witness, Jim. The first right-hand fork we come to after we take the branch road. Certain?'" he nagged.

Jesus, Wafer thought. That'll do, he decided, as well as any other. Sod them. Take the right and I'll take you right again and then again and then left and God help me so I'll show you a spot of mournful country whether it's plugged with potch or sapphire. His groin was throbbing. He hadn't managed to change the dressing for twenty-four hours and every jolt of this rougher, narrower road reminded his body of the horns. They reclaimed his groin as the rocks and scrub were reclaiming the road once they turned off into the branch, the track ahead staggering up through the hills as if it were gasping for air.

Dozing through generations of trees and only just aware of miles grinding the gravel of the road back and back, sleeping, jerking, bouncing through the pain into the full wakefulness of Cropper's elbow.

The truck had stopped.

"It's close on twenty miles," the sergeant was saying, indicating a thin trail through the trees. "You reckon this is it?"

There came the sound of the second van pulling up the slope behind them in a scatter of pebbles.

Wafer regarded the fork with only half interest. It was little more than a snigging trail from the plateau, leading into even denser scrub that argued and crowded its way to the margins.

The shy words of a poem on roads not taken.

His destiny should be more than this gloomy passage into rain. All the rupture of these last weeks. Could more matter? The girl, he wondered, why the girl dancing her saraband into diminishing landscapes?

"This is it," he lied confidently.

Cropper scowled, doubtful. "You said thirty, maybe more. Don't give us a bum lead."

Wafer leaned forward his hands on the dashboard. "Here," he insisted. "Here. For Christ's sake, here."

Cropper banged open the driving door, stepped into the drizzle and walked back to our truck into Stobo's grin.

"He says this is it. Says."

He spotted me then and bounded round the side of the truck, his eyes snapping. "What the hell's this?"

He could hardly contain his fury. But it was too late to do anything about me, the insolent stare I gave him or Jam's babbled excuses. I was aware of Wafer turning a bleak smile on me through the back cabin window and raising one hand in a nonsense wave. I waved back fraudulently as part of my jockeyship and thought, first person active voice autobiographically, "I am turning it out."

The front truck filled again, doors slammed and with Jam's shrug and a couple of horn-blasts the little convoy got under way and set off down the soaking snig trail.

Wafer must have been becoming obsessed with his myth.

There he was, jammed between law and order, a bonded leader of men wryly hoeing away into the desert with the disciples packed close and the promised land as much a mystery to himself as to the rest of us. He didn't care whether they found something or nothing. If they did make a strike it would be one of those jocular miracles that would quieten them and leave him to his personal oblivion.

He wanted that. I should have wanted it for him but saw in my inner and angry eye a road that led to some deserted cocky's patch where the folly would explode all about him.

Surprisingly, after the track's churlish beginnings, within a few hundred yards the trees moved aside and the track became a road of sorts, crawled up another line of hill, fell over the crest and staggered into a narrow valley where spewed up boulders hung between the scaffolding of the forest. At the end of this valley the road branched again.

Left or right? Wafer thought quickly. He could make any choice at all.

"Right," he said. "Right". He smiled at the thought of this innocent new map he was charting, pegging out with randomly disposed lies, the new Digger's Baedeker. He looked at his watch. They'd been on the road nearly two hours. "Not far now, as I remember," he lied again. And added with confidence. "There should be another turning about five miles on."

After all an Odyssey of untruth should offer credence.

Cropper seemed sufficiently soothed, relaxing enough

to grunt approval. "Knew you'd recall, mate, once we got on the way. Nothing like reconstructing the scene of the crime."

Both trucks were labouring over the poor grades. The rain began again in bursts, slanting across a landscape that held all the dissonant chords of human grief. We plunged deeply into the range basin, crossed creek after creek, trundling across log-spanners that rolled under the weight.

"Didn't know we had these tracks in the shire," Brim commented.

"You have to look," Wafer said mockingly. "You've got to look to find this sort of place."

Inexpressibly feeling better. The pain easing in his groin. The dead tiredness lifting in the adrenalin surge of the absurdity of this goose-chase that he would embroider and embroider with tantalizers.

But he was wrong about the turning.

Five miles. Six. Seven.

"You sure you got it right?"

Wafer examined Cropper who had begun to smoke with a nervous unenjoyment.

"You have to remember," he said carefully, "it's more than two years – nearly three – since I was here. I could be wrong about the mileage."

Yet there was his jocular miracle, almost as he spoke.

The next swing of the track showed a small side-road that lumbered up onto the hips of the range into country more inflexible and boulder-humped than that they had left. Great mounds of basalt and dolerite sulked on the scarps each side of the track, still silenced from the explosion that had flung them there, holding themselves close with embedded memories that went back, Wafer thought, to the time when Cropper was a string of slime smeared at the sea's edge.

About him, the landscape became the landscape of his

dream, riding back to him now so distinctly his guts contracted with recognition. Up, up, the road went climbing along the shoulder of the range until at last a clearing and below in a gorge dark with trees, dark with rain, the waters of a small creek slid across slabs of granite and dropped noisily into a sand-beached pool, moved on and fell out of sight beyond a spur.

"It was here," Wafer said, surprised by the authority in his voice.

There was certainly something here, if only the negatives of a dream that might or might not be the truth of the matter.

"I was camped down there by the creek," he said. "Just over there on the sand-spit."

His dream could have been as singular as a floater, as the lump of sapphire he had picked up somewhere else.

He was beginning to believe himself, his lies, the place.

What candid regrets for a life of honest dealing, he thought, watching the smacking eagerness all the greedy buggers showed as they heaved themselves out of the trucks and glared, almost, down the incline at the water.

"You quite sure?" Cropper's eyes were small with doubt. He let the rest of them pull ahead as they began to stagger and skid down the slope.

"Perfectly sure," Wafer said catching my lingering eye. And he was. Sure now as he had never been with his mother, Ruth, his uncle.

Through the grey scrub across the creek he could see the solemn disturbance of Emmie's dance.

He made his lie heroic. "You'll find my old camp-site if the rains haven't washed it out."

Below the road lip the tree canopy shut out wind and light catching slow rain and grey clouds. There was only the rattle of the creek. No birds clattered through the watching trees.

Stobo suggested a short break for lunch and I heard Brim say to Wafer that perhaps, for luck, the billy should be boiled on the same spot. "Sacramental?" Wafer asks, and waves in the direction of some rocks on the sand-shelf.

Cropper ploughed across the spit and poked about with his foot.

"No sign of a fire here, matey."

I watched Wafer. He barely glanced at the sergeant, squatted on his hunkers and became absorbed in the poignant landscape.

Cropper repeated his remark louder.

We all watched Wafer close his eyes on the emphasis, settle down into the sand, worrying a hip-hole for himself.

"I'm a clean camper," he said, his eyes shut on us. "I always bury my embers."

I know he's laughing at us and when I see Moon and Cropper exchange a look, just for a split second, mark you, the force of natural virtue in me derives new energy from the slovenly quality of our behaviour and I smart for him, Wafer lying there grey and bone-thin. So I look hard at Moon and ask,

"Do you? Do *you* bury your embers?"

It's pleasant the way his mad eyes pause, loon in on me with the others wondering.

Count the seconds. Watch guilt refresh.

"Well, okay," Moon says at last, deciding to ignore me and turning back to Wafer. "Okay."

I have created a small force-field of terrible interest and Cropper resents even fragments outside his knowledge.

"Gear!" he roars. "Get the gear!" and Stobo and Jam scramble back up the slope to the trucks while I know, yes, know, Wafer has led us to this place through a maze of lies. I want to laugh, but with him.

They unloaded shovels and buckets and rock-hammers. There was even a small dolly. It took Stobo and Jam two trips and by that time Brim had got a fire going and the billy on and we sat around under the shelter of a large boulder while the rain spat its lonely rhythms.

I have gone back to my own square one watching Wafer asleep, drained out, looking older than father, feeling my jealous rage subside as I see him there, caged in by the town. What am I doing here in this damp forest? I know I have come to see his downfall, but for those few moments I wanted nothing of that, could forget his seeming indifference and abstract only the mildness of a human who truly wished for singleness. We had hemmed him in with our demands and they had holed him out like years.

I move on from square one.

Cropper empties his mug, wipes his mouth and shakes Wafer awake.

"Right," he says into Wafer's lost face. "Enough kip for the moment. Now let's get this straight. There's a lot of country round here. Just exactly, now, where did you pick up that rock of yours? Were you up on the slope or here or what? Christ, if you were up among the rocks, there could be a whole pipe of the stuff."

Five pairs of eyes. They were boring into him as if the vitality of their combined pressure should give a tonic jog to his memory.

Wafer looked extraordinarily sad and shook his head.

"Not on the slope. Not there." The eyes formed a ring about him and he swayed. The faces had the same intensely personal eager look of those other faces, that other time.

"Well, where, man?"

Wafer licked his lips. All the cheerful light seemed to be leeched out of his countenance, draining away, drain-

ing downstream with the little waterfall, into the un-
ending mournfulness of trees.

"It was absurd, really," he said. He began to remember
how it had really happened, anywhere else at all.

"What was?"

"The way I found it. I'd just gone down to that pool
there" — we all turned to look at the pool. What a pup-
peteer, I thought — "and I was simply filling up the billy
when I saw this glint under a rock on the far bank."

"Just like that?"

"Just like that. No more and no less than that."

For after all, it had been much like that. His lies took
on a virtuous flush because there had been a creek, a
camp-fire and a gleam below water.

"Not possible!" Moon cried savagely. "Not bloody
possible. That sort of stone isn't alluvial. You're lying."

"Wait a minute," Stobo interrupted, old peacemaker.
"Just wait a minute. You're not always right. It could
have been a washdown from the cliff, a fall from up
there. It's not impossible. It could have washed down in
the rains from anywhere along this creek-bed — and this
is a seasonal creek, remember. What we have to do is
split up and start spalling. If he found it in a patch of
scree it was probably a floater, but in the creek, that's
different. We'd better split up into pairs so we can cover
more territory up and down this gully."

I was slipping into unfitting distractions as if gassed by
nostalgia with the rain dabbing endlessly at the sand, the
water, cracking on leaves; was swept into a long-lost
summer swoon of hot evenings on the station verandah
listening to the terrible properties of some amateur
baritone exploring "The Road to Mandalay", mother
leaning forward in the yellow circle of lamp-light, her
head craning short-sightedly at the music and taking my
irritation down the steps into the scented twilight, half-
crying. At what?

I had talked about this to Wafer trying to explain how my mouth or my fingers were stuffed with sound or colour and that all that came out even though I felt it high in my skull and all through my body was off-tune achromous gruel, thin and watery. The hitch between the imagining and the act. The awful gap between the feeling and the execution.

"We all fail," he had said. "We fail each other."

"Do we?"

"Oh all the time. You've a passion for the grand passion." (Hitting home!) "And what do I want? All I want is to turn away. I can be reliable and punctual and practical but I want to turn away. You don't want practicality, do you, does anyone, in the middle of a grand passion or even a grand execution? You bark your shins on your gift, you spill things in the midst of elegance. You are," he said and kindly, "the dropped hem on the billowing coat of passion."

I'd called him a pretentious shit, then, for his phrasing rather than what he said. What he said was true.

We are all failing each other right now.

The group splits into hunter couples. Stobo and Brim decide to work up the western banks of the creek; Cropper and Moon are to work the other side. They stand staring at Wafer who had dozed off again.

"Not much use taking this bugger," Cropper said. "Nothing but a handicap."

"What about these two?" Moon looked boldly at Jam and me, as if he couldn't trust us not to spirit Wafer off in one of the trucks. Although the idea had crossed my mind, something made me want to see the day through to whatever end it might take.

Jam said, "We'll work the western bank downstream. Not that Gab will be much use either, but she can hand me the tools."

We crossed the creek below the fall and started to

move away along the bankside, heading towards the rock-face. It was heavily fissured and tumbled heaps of scree lay all along the base. Cropper watched us sullenly then turned away with Moon to a natural pipe running down the cliff. Almost at once the ringing of his pick commenced and Jam steered me farther along, beyond sight of them and held out the sample bag for me to take.

"Do you really think this is the place, sis?" he asked.

To my shame, I merely shrug.

An hour has gone by. The rain has eased and the hunters are only audible as rock-strikes, word-noise fading, the snap of a branch.

Gradually, gradually, I move away from the absorbed Jam, put leafy distance between myself and the others to cross back over the creek to the fire-site. Wafer is sitting up rolling himself a cigarette.

He looks at me amusedly. That is not enough. It is, stupidly, total concern I want with memories of Torben, of Willi, of Sam, of Jackson. All he says is "Found Eldorado?" and when I tell him he knows that we won't a kind of shadow moves from his face and he laughs.

"Do I?"

"Of course you do."

"Life is one long search," he says sententiously and grinning. We have a little giggle together and the day seems to refresh itself and shower me with a light that breaks from joke-sharing or hand-touching or even the glance from strangers in the street.

"It will be bad when they realize," I say.

But neither of us realizes how bad so after a while in the companionable quality of early afternoon, I brew up another lot of tea and despite myself, despite resolutions, think of Emmie and Wafer and the note he had written her and Emmie and Moon and Wafer again and

177

Moon pacing through a riot of fire and two ruined houses.

Does Wafer know?

Have the men kept it from him?

"You're quiet," Wafer says. "Something up?"

"Just thinking."

"Tell me. If you want to, that is."

I have been a traitor and here is my chance to confess and be shriven. I assume forgiveness as automatic, old sunny-faced-I-did-it-miss of the junior school. I open my mouth to hawk out words, then choke into silence.

"Come on," Wafer says. "No good bottling it up."

So I told him.

I told him about the fire and Moon and the ruin at the lake and how I might have stopped Moon destroying Smiler's or reported it but didn't. But didn't. The whole rotten business fell out of my mouth in lumps, the whole of it except for the finding of his note. So that after a while I found myself wordless, scrawling stupid patterns with one finger in the river-sand that took no impression but just kept falling away.

Wafer wore the smile of the very last martyr, punched silly by circumstance.

"I would never have gone back there, you know," he said at last. "Not after all of this. So no matter. I'm not one of your facers-up to, nothing of that in me. And it really doesn't matter about my place, not matter at all. But poor old Colley and Emmie."

He ran a tired hand through tired hair. "That was all they had. They didn't have much — except his phoniness and her pride. My God, what pride!" He mouthed something, looking away up the creek to the falls. "I left Emmie a note. Just a goodbye note. She'll never get it now."

"No," I agreed. "Not now."

My emphasis?

His eyes became bleak as they fastened on me. "You misunderstand," he said softly. He began to explain the runic quality she had for him, a symbol of things young and past, and as he tried to tell me this, something in me refused totally to understand or, if there were danger that I might, rejected vigorously, and the next minute the hunters were back and Cropper's frustration broke over us.

"Stuck there on your arses." He was full of contempt.

"I'm not the one looking." Wafer flicked ash from his cigarette and if Cropper read insolence in the movement, I translated a last-ditch despair.

Wafer sighed. "What are you going to do? Shoot me? I've done what I said I'd do. I've shown you the place. I can't do any more, don't you see? I know nothing about fossicking, rocks, any of that stuff. I can't tell one stone from another. It would be the most terrible waste of time. Yours and mine. You'd only have to go over any patch I covered."

"You knew what to pick up, you bastard."

He strode over to us, one hand resting on the confident butt of his gun, his neck swollen and meaty. Deliberately he stared at Wafer, swept his eyes onto me for a second; then, boldly holding Wafer's eye, Cropper unzipped his flies, took out his penis and urinated onto Wafer's boots.

There was a lot of splashing and misdirection.

I began shouting my disgust, but Cropper grinned, zipped up and Wafer, stoic Wafer endured it like a mad saint.

"Okay," Cropper said, apparently calmed, "we're taking a breather and then we're trying the scarp down creek on this side. You coming or not?"

"You've made it impossible to stay here," Wafer said, wrinkling a fastidious mouth, and he picked up the rock hammer they had slung him when he first got out of the truck. Straight away he began limping off down the creek at the base of the cliff.

Cropper started roaring again. "Wait! You bloody wait till we're all ready, do you hear? I don't trust you. Jesus, I don't."

More tea, taken in silence. Then we began to move off, Stobo with Wafer and me tagging. Cropper's irritation rose as he watched Wafer, still in sight of the spit, idly swing, chip, and move on, flakes and chunks dropping at his feet without a pause to examine them.

"You taste it, bite it, cradle it in your hand for weight." Freddie Stobo had been saying in the van on the way up. "There's no limit to what you do to assess a find. Good rock men can almost smell 'em out."

Wafer neither cradled, bit nor tasted.

But I worked alongside him, persisting in the farce, trying to rip the stillness of the gully apart with my pick so that the tree barricades of this particular slammer could burst open under onslaught; so I could force Wafer into some kind of admitted confidence. I was properly humbled by now. I'd settle for my name spoken, a verbal gesture we were two of a side.

Moon came after us, panther-soft, and was watching as Wafer slung his listless pick.

"You're not very methodical, are you?" He sprang lightly over the rocks towards us. "You don't seem to give a stuff."

"Should I?" Wafer asked without looking up.

"In your boots I would. Your pissed on boots."

"But I'm not the hunter."

"You're certainly not that." Moon smiled, his frightful good looks heightened by sweat glister. "Amigo," he said. "No. You're certainly not that."

It is four o'clock.

Cropper has summoned us all at the beach spit by a signal blast on his police whistle.

Stobo had taken Wafer back there earlier. The crawling up and down banks had opened up the wound and a slow ooze showed even through his trousers.

Watching him limp away I knew I should have felt more than remorse, more than guilt. A blindingly lit charity should have scalded clean my inner corners, I know now, but then, having received no shriving, no comfort, even bogus, for my confession, I watched him go as I had watched Torben, Willi, Jackson.

They were downing beers and their sample bags had been emptied onto the sand while they stood around, draining stumpies and examining their hopeful bits of rock.

Councillor Brim, council chambers forgotten, was boyish about a strike Jam had made in a gully beyond the creek.

Jam held out a lump streaked with veins of dark translucent blue.

"It's not much," he apologized, grinning his pleasure, "but Fred's got something interesting. Show them, Fred."

Stobo dug in his pocket for this and pulled out a very

small stone that he held to catch the light. There were hints of flame.

The men became silent, crowding in on him.

Finally Cropper thrust out an ardent paw.

"Show me."

He turned the stone over with one finger as it rested on his palm, flicked it, held it up at the losing sky and tossed it up and down lightly in his hand. Finally he put it between his teeth like a nut and bit.

"Rock crystal," he said.

"Ah crap!" Stobo cried, reaching out for it. "It's not crystal, for crying out loud. Take a look at the shape."

He held it up again between thumb and forefinger rotating it slowly so that lights sprang from its axial centre, lights that burned through carmine and indigo signals which only underlined the soul of the stone.

"See!" he said triumphantly. "It's almost a bloody sphere. Eight bloody faces. And look. If I run my nail across each face I can feel smaller ones curved in a bit. You don't get crystal like that."

To me the stone had a slightly greasy look but there was that elusive glitter under the skin of it.

"Give it to me," Moon demanded. He seemed to be quivering in his nervous brown skin. He, too, put it between his teeth and cracked at it, then he spat it out onto his palm. He held it up and revolved it slowly. "I think you're right," he said.

Cropper snapped, "Don't think. Don't for God's sake think. Spell it out to us poor sods, eh."

The beer was forgotten.

"Well, look," Moon said moving over to Cropper. "It's the shape of the stone and above all the hardness that's the first guide here, anyway. Right? If it were rock crystal it would have a square-ish kind of face. There's nothing like that here."

"You both seem to know a bloody lot about it,"

Cropper said sulkily, silkily. "What do you think the damn thing is?"

"Diamond."

Wafer suddenly laughed loudly.

"Danke," he said, "grazie, tak, merci, gracias."

"And what's that wog talk supposed to mean?" Cropper demanded.

"Oh nothing," Wafer babbled. "Nothing." Bent over with pain and laughter. "A prayer maybe."

"Jesus!" Cropper said disgustedly.

Brim said doubtfully, "It could be sapphire," ignoring both of them. "Couldn't it?"

"No," Moon replied shortly. "For the same reason it's not rock crystal."

He held it up again in the faded afternoon and its heart spun into life. Moon gasped at the twinning; the urgency in both stone and man became a split of dazzling blue. Deliberately he turned towards Wafer who, holding a mug of tea and taking indifferent sips, had sat with his amusement. They all looked at Wafer, make-shift warders in Wafer's prison of creek and tree.

"And what do you think?"

"I've told you," he said. "I don't. I don't know anything at all about this — this sort of thing. Why won't you believe me?" He examined the expectant crystals of their eyes. "Oh I could give you names, fellers." He began to laugh again. "All the poetry of it. Chalcedony, jasper, carnelian, beryl." He began an amused intoning, mocking the lot of us as he savoured each word. "Azurite, turquoise, tourmaline, cairngorm, chrysoprase, garnet, sardonyx, zircon . . . " He repeated "zircon" and left it with a query hanging like a transparent eye in the slowed air.

The rain had stopped.

"It's not a bloody zircon," Stobo said impatiently. "I

know a bit about these things. It's damn well carbon. It's diamond."

"That sounds," Wafer said slowly and to irritate them, "such a cliché. Such a decadent gag yarn cliché. Oh do say carbon again, will you, and always. Carbon is a girl's best friend. It's not your best friend, is it, Gabby?" His laughter had a pale sound to it and Cropper, unable to control himself, bent over and flicked the side of his skull lightly with the backs of his fingers.

"Gum up!"

"The point is," Moon insisted, his mind narrowed into the matter as if he still wore horns, "whether we're going to keep churning about these rocks for sapphire or get up the creek to where Stobo struck this and concentrate on that. It doesn't seem to me as if pal Wafer is doing anything about opening up a little bonanza. If it was ever there."

"You want me to keep repeating, do you?" Wafer looked mildly up at Moon. "You want me to go on saying it and saying it. There was no bonanza, as you put it. An accidental solitary find. I didn't know it was sapphire. Repeat, didn't know. I don't," he said with emphasis, "care if it's a blue-arsed ossified baboon turd. I simply liked it."

My lone cluck of laughter made Cropper swing about as if he would strike me as well, while Wafer refused the energy of my amusement staring past me carefully as if I were one of the gaolers. Which I was. I suppose I was. Why else was I there?

Cropper suggested they take another look at Wafer's luck and Wafer gave him one of those direct Colley looks, straight between the eyes and said "impossible".

"Where is it?"

"It's locked in the van back at Jericho Crossing."

Was that the right lie?

I wondered. Jericho Crossing. One of those words

with all the evocations of those other names like Isfahan, Samarkand, the golden lettering across childhood pages of onion turrets, oil jars, over-detailed carpets and impossible sunsets. Jericho with a Biblical Harry James belting it out until slabs of stone tumbled down their own diatonic scales and crashed into discordances. But not this name. Not now. Not that shabby one-streeter pocked with scabby houses and native figs and a railway station that came alive twice a week. It would never be illumined by the light of that sapphire. When he had come back from hospital, on impulse he had given it to Emmie. I watched him. "My luck," he had told her sober, listening face, "appears to have run out. You take it," he had said. "Infuse new virtue."

I found myself going sullen. Where was my luck then? Where?

The men kept arguing tactics. There were words — too many — creek gravels, ridges, and My God, a pipe of the stuff someone said and only another hour of light, Jam's voice saying kimberlite and Stobo saying gawd the boy wonder and I really heard none of it, holding back the pipeline of my own tears.

All those years I had been searching humbled me. The only gentleness I ever found was in people who could do nothing for me in the way society would want: Archie Wetters gone now, Rosie Wonga in a tin humpy the town hated me to enter. Used, I kept saying to myself, used. Torben, Willi, Sam, Jackson, fraudulent time-fillers. All those injunctions about receiving, getting back what you had put in, hadn't worked for me. Wafer, you don't even have to smile. The briefest look will do. The half glance that confirms the residue of our acquaintance.

Nothing.

The rain again. The ripping paper sound of water.

And there was the sound of empties hitting the rocks.

"Okay boys," Cropper was saying, his shrunken khaki stretched tight over regulation muscles. "One more hour then. The light's almost gone and we'll have to head back. The thing is, we've got the place."

Moon's face was wolfish.

"If," he said. "If."

Wafer, now's your time to accuse. He looks at Moon and he gives a small shrug. I agree, really. What is the point?

The men pan out along the creek banks into the darkening air.

Their avarice is like a lewd golden rose.

The last light dribbled in ribbons from the tops of trees, the faintest of lemon strings as the hands of the clock and the lost sun tipped forward into six o'clock and a future burning. Being, that sun, always being, without the darks of sleep.

They left Wafer and me behind beside the ashes of our small fire in the pre-night insect buzz. The creek seemed to be running on the spot and nothing lit our stage but the gradually purpling air and the sharp cracks of picks away in the rift downstream.

There was a question I must ask but the words would not form, not in any coherent way.

Finally I managed one word. Only one.

"Emmie," I said.

Wafer turned his mild eyes on me.

"She wasn't mine," he said. "That's what you want to know, isn't it? Not mine the way you mean. But in other ways, maybe. Maybe."

Too easy. Too glib for my fanatic state.

"You made her yours." I bit my lip as I said that — could have bitten my tongue — yet I couldn't stop myself adding, "Deliberately."

"I don't know what you mean."

"Oh you know. You know. You turned her into a small

disciple, hanging on everything you said, did, even looked."

"And you," he said unkindly and unnecessarily.

"Yes," I said. "yes yes yes." Starting to cry. I've always despised tears as an old female trick but mine weren't that. They came without the asking.

"I've never had much," Wafer said, ignoring those tears, "in the way of women. Once. Oh I don't count those stray physical urgings that meant nothing. But there was one, once. I've told you about her."

"Don't try to wring me out," I begged. "Don't try that pitiful stuff. You need no one."

"I've told you that. Told you. There you go, misconstruing all the time. A painter with crossed eyes. And colour blind." He looked infinitely wearily. "I didn't *make* her into a disciple, as you put it. I didn't create the situation, not with any deliberation. I've never made anyone do anything. Never managed it. If she liked me, that was my blessing."

Then I said it. I don't know what made me. I didn't even mean it.

What was it that had always nagged in my short, sketchy relationship with Wafer? I'd known but pushed the thoughts aside as whimsy, sentiment, the juices of my female biology. The thought remained a persistent caller. I had wanted his child.

"Pederast," I accused softly, so softly I hardly heard myself say the word.

He looked as if I had struck him. I achieved notice, of a kind, but that was not enough.

"That letter," I went on. "That note you wrote her. It was still there, blazing on the grass, you might say." Words and crazier accusations came rushing out of me. "I read it. Oh I'm still reading it. It told me the lot. The lot."

Still he said nothing.

I raced to my doom. "I tore it up, do you hear? I tore it into the smallest pieces known to man, again and again. So tiny, so tiny, it was molecules and atoms."

The creek seemed to speak for both of us.

"Go away," Wafer said at last. "Please go away. I'd thought you had — well — sensibility. I thought there was a chance for you. You had, I thought, fresh ideas. Wrong. Wrong. You haven't. You're as stale and square and conventional as those pot-bellies cracking at rocks down there. I can forgive any of the wild things you said. I know you don't mean them. Even for destroying that note. For watching their home blaze. All of that. But you haven't enough sensitivity to understand *how* I can. You haven't the maturity to know that in a little while, a very little while, Emmie would have forgotten all about me. That's the way it is. Perhaps," he went on saying across and through my half-words of interruption, "she might have been influenced but she would have forgotten the influencer. Almost forgotten. And you can't understand that. You really can't. The sad thing is, Gabby, you never will."

That gagged me. There wasn't even contempt in his voice. Only disappointment and pity, and a terrible boredom.

"Please go away," he said.

I looked.

His eyes were closed, shutting me out for ever and in with my self-disgust.

When I caught up with the others, galloping on my shame, the rain began belting the whole world.

Cropper was saying, "This seems a waste of time. A hell of a waste of time. There's nothing here. Nothing except mud and gravel. Let's pack it in!"

Jam kept arguing for Stobo's find.

"That's no diamond," Cropper said spitefully. He was soaked through, hungry and feeling a bit of a charley. "Probably is zircon. That bugger knows more than he'll admit."

Although they had moved into the shelter of the cliffs the rain kept driving in on them, enforcing closeness.

"You've abandoned your saint," Moon said softly as I came up. "I bet he's having a laugh. Didn't I keep telling you," he went on, swinging towards Cropper. "Didn't I warn you? You don't damn well listen."

"Jesus," Cropper said, "I do nothing but listen in my job. You're only a tenth part of the general moans, mate. I'm one godawful ear. How the hell can I tell between fact and fiction, eh? How? Can you?"

The rain stopped suddenly but the trees kept dripping, dripping.

"Come on," Stobo urged. "Let's get back to the trucks while there's a break. We can't keep frigging around here. By the time we get back Doss'll be fit to tie. I'll go stir him up and follow you."

"Just a minute," I said. I was numbed by what I was about to do. My last betrayal was choking me.

The five faces swung like unfriendly masks.

"You've been wasting your time, you lot," I said.

A golden circle, my mind raged. A circle I could never comprehend. I am turning it out. Over. Over.

"This isn't the place."

They didn't ask me how I knew. They kept looking at me. Their faces said they didn't think much of me either, I could tell.

"He told me," I said.

Footsteps, spaced and heavy, were crunching bracken and forcing their way up the bank below Wafer who had crawled under a rock-shoulder when the heavy rain broke.

He had been hearing them yell his name; even the blasts on Cropper's whistle failed to budge him, and he kept squatting there in a kind of stupor. Why bother to answer? Go? Move? He rejected the idea of returning with them but doubted he could manage the miles and miles of hike to the bitumen.. And even if he did? What then? Even if he managed a hitch, even if he made it to the coast, their noxious charge, fragile as it was, could pursue him until life became a jungle of charge and counter-charge. A form of human radiation.

Or would they bother? Were they really childish or venomous enough to bother?

At the end of it all, merely to sit and to keep sitting.

Boots appeared.

Stobo was standing above and to one side of the shelf, looking down and not grinning for once.

"Okay," he said abruptly. "You want to stop here? We're shoving off."

Wafer kept snapping at the twig he had been playing with, mathematically halving until he could break it no further. Like his little note. He felt strange, dissociated.

One side of his head kept hearing the sedate music of the saraband running in streamers through the sunless trees.

"Well?"

He looked up at this unsmiling chap.

"I don't know. I truly don't know."

"Oh come on, you silly bugger." Stobo soon forgot grudges. Kindness came easier. "You'd better come. Stuck here with that leg and all." He hesitated. "They think you've given them a bum steer. You have, haven't you?"

Stobo's eyes were frankly curious now, rather than angry. There was even some amusement. He rubbed a hand through his sopping thatch and suddenly he couldn't stop his grin. "You old bastard," he said.

Wafer examined the grin and still huddled in the part comfort of the rock grinned back.

"It wasn't deliberate." Stobo waited. "I really couldn't remember, but you all seemed to want me to produce something, so I produced. One place is much like another out here, isn't it?"

"Not if you're frenzied," Stobo said, "as they are. As I was. We're all greedy."

Wafer gazing down through the tree scramble, the humped backs of sleeping granite to the inky creek shine hesitating between its banks, sought behind the very fabric of his mind.

"I still don't know," he said, "where I found the damn thing. It's as if I've blocked it totally out. But all you wanted was a place. A place. That was the thing, wasn't it? The idea of discovery?"

"Not quite," Stobo said gently.

"And I don't know," Wafer went on, "I don't know either if I want to go back with you. You've stymied me, somehow. I just want" — and he used the obscenity as if

192

he were spitting something vile from his tongue — "to be shat of the lot of you."

Stobo looked idiotically hurt. He shrugged.

"Don't play silly buggers," he said, not unkindly, "not in this goddam weather. Come on up. I'll see they play okay."

Wafer eased himself up, caught at the rock face, teetered, straightened and rubbed his backside, hedging for time. Carefully he picked a few burrs caught in his sleeves.

Shouts came from higher up near the road rim, impatient yells. Someone blasted a car-horn.

"All right," he said reluctantly. He resolved to follow Emmie's measured dance steps right to the back of the stage.

Stobo gave a shout and they started up the slope pushing through the dark wet air. Below them, the creek fed from higher up the range, made its own impatient noises, gobbling the same sounds again and again as it licked twilight like paste into sand, into shelving banks, over the greened stones above the rapids.

Wafer limped back, with Stobo helping him, into our rancorous circle and by now all I wanted was his ruin.

Cropper had me travel back with him. Wafer was crushed between us and in the back of the van Moon was wound for a strike.

I was punished every way.

Wafer's tense profile seemed to gather in the diminishing road as we climbed from the valley's dusk, crawling through water now at the plank crossings, sliding and gripping at the mud of the track.

No one spoke for the hour it took to reach the turn-off

and my resentment had lost track of time. As Wafer said, it was for me still four o'clock by the sand spit.

It was only when the van went into a skid on the branch-road that Cropper broke the silence. As he tried to pull the van back onto the gravel, the back wheels churned so deeply into the mud that in a raging silence forced out, flashing his torch about, he dragged a couple of fallen boughs back to the road and shoved them in behind the wheels. Still raging he climbed back in, opened up the motor and heard the car moan as it settled into a wallow.

"You'll keep," he said to Wafer, not looking at Wafer.

I turned and saw through the cabin window-glass the demi-crescent of Moon's smile, a smile that seemed to be the bar-lines of a little song he was humming. There he is now, crouched over the dying piano at the Wowser, scribbling threats in Spanish.

Wafer said unexpectedly, "I don't feel very durable."

Moon leapt lightly from the back of the van and went to help Cropper pack more branches, wedge stones. In the absence of those two I looked for an answer to Wafer's words, would make one last try for redemption. But even as I attempted to say I was sorry, sorry, Jam's van came behind and the blaze of headlights only seemed to stimulate Cropper's fury. Savagely he waved the other van on and climbed back in again, crashing his gears into forward drive as if he would kill them. The van bucked, shuddered, bucked, and then, throwing mud wide, crawled back onto the road.

Cropper was driving his hatred.

"I like a feller," he said softly, "who understands his worth."

Behind us Moon was whistling mournfully the dodgy edges of his elegy till I thought I would go crazy with the doppelgangers of Emmie toe-ing along its score. Moon's darkness underlined the whole night world we were entering, adding the darkness, I knew, of a certain river clearing, of fire, of a black man without hands on the other side of the globe.

The world whirled.

I am Moon.

I am Cropper.

I am my father's daughter, the old man doing a Pontius Pilate as he watched the trucks pull out.

I am all of them.

"Wafer's lucky," Cropper was saying, talking straight at the wind-screen into the light path ahead. "He understands his worth. For sure. And I almost understand my own. The brevity of it. I'm not one of your sickly intellectual fart-arsers, Wafer, but I have a small worth. I value it. Those others —" He stopped. Chewed at other words. Was beginning to ramble. I suppose he was strangled by the size of Wafer's victory. I know I was. My thoughts were a chaos of reprisals through whose glades I raced like Moon, not wanting to be Moon, a starveling nemesis, a stick man of ribs, spine, arm and leg bones flailing at revenge.

Charon drives a truck these days.

We were trundling behind the nimbus of the other van, a vapour-scut that bounced along the road ahead, getting farther away, shrinking, vanishing into the dark.

Suffering fails to ennoble. I am viler than Moon who had ceased the courtesy of humming below his breath and was chanting with metallic irony, "No me queda nada nada."

I can translate that. Don't have a thing. Nothing at all. Nothing. Nothing. Does he mean himself? Wafer? The lot of us?

Not only suffering. Poverty doesn't ennoble either. There's nothing less firming than wondering where the next dinner's coming from, the next month's rent, the hire purchase instalment, the bus fare home.

195

Monstrous! The enormity of Wafer's fragile theories! I am whipping myself into a righteous rationalization of my deeds. I am scraping about for sympathy for these hunters. Suffering, poverty loss, I tell myself, ignoring the facts of Archie Wetters, of Rosie Wonga, of Wafer himself, make you malicious, debased, a traitor.

"No me queda nada nada," Moon sang.

Cropper is driving flash and fast now we are back on the coast road, his handsome thug profile in the dashboard light, sour with resolutions, I can tell, that will involve the lot of us.

Wafer's eye beside my own is expectant.

Twenty miles out of Allbut among the wrangling hills, Cropper slows the van down, lets it crawl to a stop. We are at the peak of the home range and between thinning trees I imagine I can see the bland eye of the lake. Moon's voice cuts out on an unfinished "nothing." Beside me, Wafer stiffens.

"I'm charging you," Cropper says softly. "Mate."

Wafer could not reply for strange exhilaration, aware of the foreseen moment.

His shanks felt vulnerable beneath the aching fabric of his trousers, his belly rumbled with emptiness, his head was stupefied from lack of sleep and, as he was aware of these things, his mouth went dry. They had waited for him in the change-room at his boarding-school armed with sand-shoes. His body smarted now, recalling the whacks. "You rotten little poof, Wafer," one of the older boys had cried, "dodging out on the tackle. This is to teach you not to be a rotten little poof." Someone had began to chant "no poofs here" and the others had taken it up rhythmically, whacking with each word. There

196

was his face streaked with mucous and blood peering back at him through the windscreen of forty years.

"Get out," Cropper said beside him, opening his own door and stepping onto the road.

Wafer looked up at Cropper's engorged face, glimmering in the back-glow from the headlights. He was like a mediaeval grotesque. He was the death mask carried in pageants, carnivals, funerals. The shadows lengthened the nose, obliterated the eyes. The mouth became a yawp of teeth.

Leaning back into the van, Cropper doused the lights.

Everyone reaches a point beyond which the morrow is no longer visible: despite the trees, the bulk of the sergeant, the road — a sense of blinkers. Wafer fumbled desperately along the dashboard for the car keys and then there was a terrible crack and stunning pain as Cropper crashed his gun smartly on to the wrist bone.

"Out," he repeated.

Wafer hauled himself along the seat, stumbled out the open door and took three tentative steps away from the van into the darkness. At once Moon leapt from the back of the van and slid round by the bonnet, knife-like, blocking, thrusting dark against dark, his head cracking skylines.

"I'm charging you," Cropper said, and added, strangely formal, "on two counts."

At that point Wafer began running, dragging his wounded leg distortedly, racing into the nothingness he knew was ahead.

"Get him," Cropper shouted at Moon. "Get him."

Wafer didn't know why he ran. I'm certain he didn't, for he seemed to make no progress. The road did not unwind. No trees moved back. It was as if he were running on the spot, on his Thursday, and not even the slapping and dragging of the soles of his feet reached his ears. The imprints were trackless as his body careered forward into what he knew to be a great gulf at the end of which Emmie danced with her father with increasing lightness, the gravity vanishing from her steps. "Ghostly father, I confess" he heard himself saying above the distant, the very distant dissonance of shouts.

For I was shouting, too, in those last moments; but *for* him, I swear, *for* him. And when I tried to grab Cropper's gun arm and screech an explanation, a mercy, an anything into his intransigent mug, he smacked me hard across the head and I reeled in a lather of words: "resisting arrest . . . interfering with . . . "

He left me reeling and ran past me into the dark.

He gave a warning. I suppose he gave a warning. Someone told me they are compelled to give warning.

Wafer did not seem to hear. He kept staggering down the road away from us.

Cropper's first shot missed but the second took him square between the shoulders, pitching him flat on his face.

I kept wondering why his feet kept pounding down the road, down the gulf I knew he was exploring and why the two men kept standing over him watching. I seem to be standing there too. Lying there, even.

And eventually, after a long while, after a very long while, his feet stopped slicing distance back, and confident from the no-sound of his smacking feet, I knew he had reached the place he had been racing towards.

He knew.

Move on to the last square. To Now.

I go back.

The hill is as steep but the car track out beside the dam is only just discernible and at the point where it leaves the blacktop and crosses a creek, the surface has sunk and boulders stare out.

Ten years.

Nothing has changed except the resurging waves of grass and burr. Overhead a hawk hangs in the wind and I hear Wafer say as he said so often, his eyes holding the daylight, "We have only a minute. Well, maybe two."

The orchard grove is run wild and a tangle of weed and the wind takes its course through the pines that grow from the side of the track as I walk steadily up, back to my own square one, up for one, for two hundred feet. I pick a yellow flower, a button of a thing, and am reminded of Emmie. A piece of quartz, so chalk-white, it reminds me too. And at the top, there, only a little changed by weather, the charred limbs of the house.

The hawk drops closer, flaps like a flag.

The melted records, the scorched books – they are still where the explosion dropped them, the fire caught them, scattered like Mosaic tablets for a town that has finally died. Father dead, Jam moved on, the shops and pubs closed down. Beyond this injured hillside where two ash-piles inspect each other, nothing is left.

I stand there, wondering where the others are now. Where are you Smiler, Emmeline? Where are you Doss, Fred, Moon, Sergeant Cropper, young Rider?

Nothing matters. I have never been able to face coming back before this. Never. But now I am here, there is one last thing I can do.

I go up to the ripped open shelter. Two walls at least are intact and if I drag bits of iron across the gape there will be some kind of roofing.

I climb down the crumbling concrete and get out my note-book. Then carefully, in my very best handwriting, I write down word for word, Wafer's note to Emmie. I fold it carefully and put it under a small piece of stone.

There's nothing more to do.

I sit down and wait.